GWYNETH IN THE GARDEN

AMANDA GALE

Brenda
&Cobern

for my teachers

CONTENTS

CHAPTER ONE

The first time she noticed the men, she was stepping out of her bathtub.

It was an antique claw foot tub, an original to the house, and she'd been indulging in a languid mint-scented bath. She'd just wrapped her silvering red hair in a towel when movement outside the window made her jump and cry out. She crouched naked on the floor to avoid being seen, then pulled the curtains shut before scuttling out of view toward her bathrobe.

Once decent, she crept toward the window. Tentatively she peeled back the curtain and tilted her head just enough to gaze outside.

About half a dozen men were standing about in the overgrown lot next door. Gwyneth watched them with interest. It was odd to see men next door—to see anyone, as the house, the only other house on this lonely rural road, had been abandoned for many years. These men were talking in a circle, some with their arms folded, some pointing this way and that. They all looked at the surroundings—the ancient oaks with the crumbling bark, the rickety barn that was covered with moss, the house with the

1

boarded-up windows, looming silently in the background like a sullen old man resigned to his death. The once proud turret was decrepit and sad, with broken shingles and chipping paint. It was September, and the leaves were already touched with red, orange, and gold. It was, according to Leona, going to be a cold, early winter. As Gwyneth peered at the subtly graying landscape, she could sense the earth's oncoming hibernation.

Gwyneth stood securely hidden behind the curtain. Unobserved, she allowed her eyes to take in the details of these men. They were youngish men, and by that she meant, younger than she. They were largely strong and well-built, and their clothes, mostly jeans and flannels and sweatshirts, suggested hard work. A couple of them had beards. These men were rugged and rough, and enjoyable to look at. Her eyes roved freely, with a little twittering thrill. It was a certain power, somehow, the liberties one might take when invisible.

And just as she was thinking that, one of the men lifted his gaze to her window. Gwyneth jumped back, startled and unnerved. She tucked her chin and pulled her robe tighter, then glided into her bedroom to dress for her day at work.

WHEN SHE RETURNED HOME that afternoon, they were still there.

She'd already surmised that they were there to clear the land and renovate the house, and she was right. As she pulled into her driveway and gathered her purse, she leaned into the passenger's seat to watch them working. One of the men was running some kind of heavy machinery over the overgrowth, leaving soft, tilled earth in its wake. Two other men were removing the rotted cedar siding, revealing the crumbling frame underneath. Yet another was sitting on the top step of the porch, appearing to study a paper on a clipboard. His head was bent over his work, and his blond hair fell in crests over his temples. Every second or so, he wrote something down or crossed something out.

Gwyneth stepped out of her car and quietly shut the door. Then she hurried up her front steps and into her house, on soft, light feet, avoiding their gazes.

She dropped her purse on a little table and went to the window at the bottom of the stairs, pulling her scarf tighter around her throat to stave off the chill of her drafty Victorian house. She was risking being seen, here on the first floor, but she was curious—not only about the men, but about the goings-on at that house. At work, she'd asked Leona if the plot had been sold, and Leona had told her all she knew.

"Liam Baxter's his name," she'd said, magnifying glass in hand, staring at one of dozens of sepia photographs on her oversized cluttered desk. Her once-gold pixie cut hair was disheveled, as usual, and the busy patterns on her oversized sweater brought a burst of color to the otherwise understated room. "From Boston. He's got permits out the wazoo."

"Permits? What for?"

"For everything." Leona had put the magnifying glass down and taken a long sip from the gas station paper coffee cup beside her. "For electrical, for new roof layout, for knocking down walls. Must be wicked expensive."

Gwyneth had crossed her arms and gazed out the window that looked onto Main Street, thinking. "I wonder why a man would leave Boston to move into an old house here in Dearham."

"Because this is the life, that's why." Leona drained her coffee, then, with a satisfied sigh, threw the cup in the direction of the trash bin in the corner; it landed with a clunk on the floor. She leaned back in her chair and stretched, then picked up the magnifying glass and resumed her work. "Just look at this town. Just look at those mountains." She gestured with the magnifying glass toward the window. "Who wouldn't want to live here?"

As Gwyneth had returned to her desk, she'd considered what

Leona had said. Though she'd lived on this little Maine isle for almost thirty years, and though she cherished the safety and comfort of her charming small town, she could imagine the allure of the city, where nobody knew who you were, where you could start from scratch and reinvent yourself.

The doorbell rang, and Gwyneth jumped out of her reverie. Heart pounding, she abandoned the window and tiptoed toward the door, the old wooden planks creaking under her boots.

She peered warily out the peephole.

It was a man, a tall one, the blond one from next door, the one who'd been writing on his clipboard. He didn't have his clipboard now; he was standing with his hands in the pockets of his dusty black parka, patiently waiting.

Gwyneth so rarely had visitors. What did he want with her?

She straightened her disobedient hair in its long ponytail. Then she cracked the door open and peeked cautiously outside. "Yes?"

"Good afternoon, ma'am," the man said. "I'm Nick. I'm the contractor working on the house next door. How are you today?"

His voice was quiet, but friendly; it was softer than she had expected. Gwyneth relaxed and met his eyes. "I'm well."

He smiled, his eyes crinkling in the corners. He watched her through the crack in the door, presumably waiting for her to open it wider. Warily, she did so, enough for them to be able to talk more easily, but not so much that she couldn't slam it shut quickly.

He said, "I just wanted to let you know we'll be out there pretty much all day for a couple of months. We'll try not to impose on you too much."

"Oh," said Gwyneth, glancing outside at the men next door, relaxing further. "That's very nice of you."

"The project's pretty big," he went on. "The entire place has to be renovated and restored, and the yard has to be dug up and replanted. It'll probably get pretty noisy over there." A polite smile crossed his face. "If we're disturbing you too late or too early, please don't hesitate to let us know."

Gwyneth allowed herself to return his smile, and she blinked a few times, a little coquettishly. "I won't."

"The good news is, after we're through, the house'll be really nice. I'll bet you'll enjoy the view."

Gwyneth's eyes darted toward the men swarming around the house, then back to Nick's angular features and golden blond hair. "Yes, I'll enjoy the view."

"Well," he said, "thank you for your time." He smiled once more and waved. Gwyneth's eyes followed his hand, searching for a wedding ring; she spotted one, and her spirit deflated.

He backed up a step or two and turned to walk away.

"Wait," she said.

He turned back and looked at her inquiringly.

She attempted an indifferent expression and a nonchalant tone. "Do you know anything about the owner?"

"Liam?" Nick faced her fully. "He's from Boston. About my age. He's a really nice guy."

"What does he look like?"

Nick stared at her, seeming to consider. Then his face lightened slightly, a smile just touching the corners of his eyes. "Tall, slim—kind of quiet looking."

Gwyneth offered a polite smile. "Okay," she said, closing the door. "Thanks."

She stood a moment, listening to the sound of his feet pounding against the steps of her front porch. Then she shut and locked the door, pulled her scarf tighter, and stepped back toward the window. Nick was reclaiming his clipboard and walking with some of the men into the house. The others were going about their work, scrambling this way and that, their breaths now visible against the increasingly brisk evening air. She watched them for a few minutes, then took a call from Tansy, who was crying again over Ken. Then Gwyneth picked up her book from the table and sat with it in the chair by the window, listening to the sounds of the men's work just on the other side of the wall.

~

GWYNETH STOOD by the Historical Society window, gazing onto Main Street. It was quiet, as usual, only a couple of town residents visiting the dozen or so establishments in the isle's quaint downtown. She watched the trees sway in the breeze. Leaves tossed about at their feet, crusty and curled with age, like dancers past their prime.

"What time are the kids coming?" called Leona from inside her office, interrupting Gwyneth's thoughts.

"Oh," said Gwyneth, pulling tighter the tie that cinched her sweater. "One o'clock, the teacher said."

Leona grumbled and returned to her paperwork.

Gwyneth once again directed her attention to the leaves. They were rising and swirling, intermingling in the air and then tumbling back to the earth, only to be lifted again. Autumn would be swiftly drifting toward winter; already, one's boots crunched upon the early morning frost. Where do the leaves go? she wondered, her eyes following their circling motions. How many turns in the wind can they withstand before they crumple from being battered about?

The phone rang, and Gwyneth returned to her desk and answered it. It was Mr. Harlowe, from Weatherby Lane. Mr. Harlowe was writing a book about the isle, and he liked to pore through the Historical Society's photos on Tuesday afternoons.

"Who's that?" called Leona, unseen behind her office walls.

Gwyneth politely wished Mr. Harlowe a good day and hung up the phone. "Mr. Harlowe."

"His usual time?"

"His usual."

Gwyneth rested her elbows on her desk and clasped her hands together, feeling rather thoughtful, though she wasn't sure why.

"He's never going to finish that damn book," said Leona. "How long's it been, now?"

Gwyneth rubbed her lips together and furrowed her brow as she calculated. "Well," she said, "I've been working here twenty-two years. Since Tansy was in kindergarten. So I suppose it's been a little longer than that."

"Poor old coot," Leona muttered, and Gwyneth couldn't help but smile. She stood and returned to the window.

The wind picked up, and the window rattled in its frame. Gwyneth felt the cold slinking over her shoulders and down the back of her blouse like a kiss from chilled lips. It made the back of her neck prickle, and it fondled her wispy gingered hair. The leaves outside were scattering, never to see each other again.

The front door opened, and the clamor of boisterous children made her turn her head. She smiled and met them at the doorway, taking in the sight of the curious faces before her.

She clasped her hands before her waist, waiting patiently for the teacher to quiet them.

"Good afternoon, children," she told them with a smile, her low, heady voice entrancing them into silence. "Welcome to the Dearham Historical Society."

WHEN SHE RETURNED HOME, the men were at their work. Once again, she scuttled from her car and into the house, only to watch them from the window before turning inward for the remainder of the evening. The sounds of the machines, and of their voices, continued to reach her from the window, and Gwyneth listened, fascinated and comforted, as she fixed herself some dinner and puttered about her house, her bare feet creaking on the cold hard-wood floor.

After they'd gone, when the digging and drilling and crashing had ceased, she slid with a sigh into her claw foot bathtub, the curtains pulled back from the lone grand window. The full moon had risen in the indigo sky, suspended like a stage prop, its halo twinkling with the endless stars and its silver beams spilling across the bathroom floor. They crept up the side of the tub and over the fragrant water, illuminating her skin and imbuing the room with silent magic.

CHAPTER TWO

"That's too much sugar, Ma," said Tansy, grimacing as Gwyneth scooped a third spoonful into her tea.

Gwyneth closed her eyes a moment as she held her nose above the steaming cup of floral tea, and sniffed. Her soul relaxed, and she sighed. "No, it's not. It's perfect."

"I don't know how you can drink it like that. Give me a cup of strong, hard coffee any day."

Gwyneth shrugged. "I like it sweet."

"That's because you're so sweet yourself." Tansy leaned across the table and smiled at her mother, then leaned back casually in her seat. "Incidentally," she added, grinning, "strong and hard is how I like my men, too."

Gwyneth, from behind her teacup, raised her eyebrows in agreement.

"I guess that's why it didn't work out with Ken," Tansy continued, tearing up again. "He may be strong on the outside, but inside he's a scared little boy."

"He wasn't the right man for you," said Gwyneth, patting her daughter's hand; she'd been through this before and knew the best way to comfort Tansy was to indulge her.

"Maybe I'm just not meant to find the perfect man." Tansy rubbed her nose with a tissue. "I already used up all my luck with Daddy."

Gwyneth blinked a couple of times but said nothing.

"It's just so unfair I never even got to meet him," Tansy continued. She blew her nose, loudly, several times. "Ma, tell me that story again." She perked up marginally; her wide eyes sparkled, making her look to Gwyneth like she was six years old again. "You know, the one that always makes me feel better, about how you and Daddy fell in love."

Gwyneth rubbed her lips together. "Well, we met in Orchard Grove Beach on a clear, perfect day."

"You were staying there the summer after your second year of college, and he had just graduated."

"Yes." Gwyneth swallowed, then looked at her daughter and smiled. "We first saw each other at an ice cream stand on the boardwalk. I had just ordered a butter pecan cone, and when I looked up I saw he'd been staring at me. It was—"

"—endearing, and charming, and it made your heart flutter," finished Tansy, her voice regaining its usual buoyancy. "I always love that part."

Gwyneth closed her eyes. "He drifted toward me and asked if I'd like to join him. We ended up spending the day together, walking along the ocean's edge."

"It was as if you'd known each other forever."

"I knew something special was happening, even that first day. We finished—"

"—each other's sentences. You held hands that night under the—"

"—fireworks. From that moment forward—"

"—you spent every minute of the summer together. You never, ever—"

"—ever wanted to be apart."

Tansy and Gwyneth both smiled; they'd recited the story

together a thousand times, and it felt comforting, like going home.

"And that's how your romance began," said Tansy. She sighed. "It's so unfair that he was taken from you so soon."

"Yes." Gwyneth studied her daughter, this beautiful young woman she'd brought into the world. She reached across the table and took a lock of her daughter's sable-colored hair in her fingers; she twirled it a moment, thinking.

Tansy sighed again, sniffled, and shook her head to clear it. "I can't believe I let myself get hurt by Ken again. After everything. I really should have known better."

Gwyneth secretly agreed. She rubbed her shoulder but said nothing.

Tansy stared out the kitchen window and shook her head. "I should have known he'd go back to his wife."

"Any man who cheats on his wife is trash."

Tansy looked at her mother with raised eyebrows. "Ma?"

Gwyneth took a breath against the sudden pounding of her heart. "I only mean that you're such a sweet, sensitive girl. Ken was never going to be everything you needed."

"I can't believe I'm so stupid."

Gwyneth's face softened as her heart cleaved in two. She put down her teacup and now held Tansy's hand in both her own. "Don't you dare say that. That's my daughter you're talking about." She patted Tansy's hand, then firmed her jaw. "The heart wants what it wants. Resistance can be hard even if you know in your mind it isn't right." She paused a moment, choosing her words. "All you can do is take these lessons and move forward."

Tansy sighed again and nodded, a tear running down her cheek.

"You're very trusting, Tansy. It means your heart is good, even if it gets broken sometimes."

Tansy looked up at her mother and smiled tearfully. "Thanks," she uttered, wiping a tear from her face.

"I love you, sugar."

"I love you, too."

A loud crash from the house next door jarred them from this moment of intimacy, and they both jumped in their seats.

"What the hell is going on over there?" asked Tansy.

"They're tearing down that big old barn." Gwyneth withdrew her hands and leaned back in her chair with her tea. "Leona says they're going to rebuild and expand it."

"So much work for such an old, ugly house. Why does this guy want to live there, anyway? Why not just buy something new?"

"Old houses have a lot of charm, I guess. It's nice to bring these old houses back to life."

"Seems like a waste of time to me."

Another crash, and cheering from the men. Tansy stood and walked to the window by the stairs, then pulled back the gossamer curtain and watched.

"Wow."

The barn on the side of the house now had no roof, and the walls were down to the trusses. Men were scrambling about pulling off trusses, tossing them into a dumpster with glee.

"Lots of strong, hard men right there," said Gwyneth, glancing at Tansy with her gracefully curvaceous form and long straight sable hair. Tansy was chic and stylish, from her perfectly applied makeup to her high-heeled boots, and she always seemed ahead of the trends. Today she was wearing a tight low-cut dress; Gwyneth often grimaced at her daughter's immodest clothing, but she had to admit she looked fabulous. "You could take your pick."

But Tansy was shaking her head. "No, they're not my type. I like suits, not lumberjacks. On the other hand," she said, pointing, "the blond one's pretty cute."

"He's married," said Gwyneth, her voice not without firmness.

"Bummer." Tansy rubbed her lips together. "Although—"

"There's no 'although' after 'he's married,' sugar."

Another crash made them start where they stood. They

leaned farther toward the window to peer off to the side, where siding was being ripped from the house—if one could call the falling of disintegrating pieces "ripped."

Thus cuddled together, secretly spying on the men and their work, they chatted and giggled, partners in crime. Gwyneth reached her arm around her daughter's back. Her heart was happy. She didn't always mind being alone—she was in love with her house, with all its nooks and crannies, its whimsical drafts and high ceilings. It was a house for secrets, for imaginations set free. But the absence of her daughter she felt keenly.

"You need to come home more often," said Gwyneth, rubbing her daughter's back. "The house feels fuller when you're here."

Tansy laughed and let her mother pull her closer. "I live twenty minutes away, Ma," she said, accepting a kiss on the cheek. "I see you at least three times a week."

"It feels like miles between visits."

"I know." Tansy gazed outside while her mother held her. "I've had a lot of night shifts at the shop. I'll be even busier if I end up going back to school."

"I know, but it would be worth it."

Tansy was silent, thinking. "It would be great to be a nurse," she said. "But I'm kind of old to go back to school, don't you think?"

Gwyneth turned to her. "But you've been talking about being a nurse for years. I thought you were already applying to schools. Are you rethinking your decision?"

"I don't know."

Gwyneth frowned and looked outside to prevent Tansy from seeing. "I'd just hate to see you abandon your dream, sugar. You'd be a wonderful nurse, and it would be such a meaningful job."

"I like the job I have. I run the whole shop now and am making decent money. It's pretty cool that I get to look ahead at trends and stuff. Plus, I love my coworkers. It's a good job—when the owner isn't driving me nuts, which admittedly is pretty often."

"It's not a bad job."

Neither said anything for a minute or two. Outside, the men continued their work. One of them spotted them watching, and waved. Gwyneth flinched, embarrassed, but Tansy beamed and waved back.

Tansy smiled and neatened her mother's hair, tidying the graying red wisps that had escaped her ponytail. "You were lucky to have Daddy," she said. "He was so perfect. I wish I could find a man just like him."

Gwyneth's grin faded, and she shifted uncomfortably where she stood.

Tansy turned and stepped toward a little table that sat in an alcove by the stairs. She reached forward and picked up a framed photo in which a much younger Gwyneth and a man stood with their arms around each other's backs. The man was dark-haired and square-jawed—impeccably, impossibly handsome. Tansy stroked the side of his face.

"I always thought Daddy looked like Van Donnelly," Tansy said wistfully. She smiled. "He's only the most handsome actor of all time, even if he is in his fifties now."

"He sure is," Gwyneth murmured, stifling a sly grin. "Every girl I knew growing up had the biggest crush on him. I sure did."

"I can see why you haven't found anyone to replace a man who looked like him."

Gwyneth took a deep breath, still gazing outside. "I haven't had time for men."

"Yes, you have." Tansy replaced the photo and returned to her mother. She picked at her sweater, frowning disapprovingly. "You're so beautiful, Ma. Look at your nice figure, your long sexy hair. You should dress more modern. You should get out more."

"Tansy, really," said Gwyneth, turning to her daughter, provoked out of her reservation and impatient to change the subject. "This is the last thing we need to be talking about right now."

"Daddy wouldn't want you to be lonely."

Gwyneth's lips parted to say something, but she rubbed them together instead. She sighed and turned back to the window.

"I've been with men since Daddy," she reminded her. "It isn't like I'm a hermit."

"Look around, Ma."

Gwyneth sighed again and looked around her house. It was utterly, unmistakably feminine, with displays of dried flowers and floral, if understated, wallpaper and fabrics. Though tidy, the room before her was clearly lived in, by a woman of a certain age; it was strewn with shawls, teacups, and used hardcover romance novels. Her reading glasses rested where she'd left them on a lace-covered table.

"I'm just saying," said Tansy, picking her purse off the floor to head home, "you're only forty-seven. You're still young."

"I'm not that young." Gwyneth picked a container of leftovers from the table and handed it to her daughter to take home. "I'm old enough to be your mother."

"Barely."

Gwyneth playfully punched her daughter in the arm, then pulled her close for a hug. The two parted. After Tansy had closed the door behind her, Gwyneth returned to the window, hiding herself more fully now that the sun had begun to set. As she gingerly pulled back the curtain, she saw Tansy approach the men and wave goodbye, a brilliant smile on her face. A few of them paused in their work and waved back, watching her retreat a few moments before getting back to work. They packed up and left soon after. Gwyneth retired to bed.

She lay with the curtains wide open, letting the moonlight filter through the window and onto her frame beneath the sheets. She liked how the shadows intertwined with the light, how by twisting her legs this way and that she could make the light dance on her body, just so.

CHAPTER THREE

*a*s Leona had predicted, winter came early. The leaves turned to fire and gold, then crumbled and blew away or rested where they'd fallen, awaiting the oncoming snow. Gwyneth watched the house blossom as the foliage withered and died. By early November, it was complete, from the porch steps to the curving turret. The landscape was bare but tidy. The house itself looked stately and proud, but dark inside, ready to accommodate life.

Gwyneth now missed the sounds of the men outside, the knowledge they were mere feet away from her as she went about her evenings. She missed watching them from the window by the stairs or by her tub. Their lively chatter, their scurrying about the property, their little personal quirks and details had sustained her in her loneliness.

"Why is the barn so big?" Tansy had asked one day, standing with her mother by the window at the stairs. "What's the guy going to do in there?"

"Maybe he'll keep horses. Maybe it will be a work station of some sort. I don't know."

"I wonder what kind of work he's in. Maybe he keeps motorcycles."

"He's coming from Boston. Leona says he was an investment banker. I have no idea what he plans to do with that building."

Gwyneth found out, at least in part, in the first week of November as she was once again stepping out of her bathtub. She'd left the curtain open; movement from below drew her eyes toward the house, and there he was, her new neighbor, directing his movers as they heaved furniture into the house.

Gwyneth peaked out the window through an opening in the curtains, the curiosity a physical ache in her blood. She'd just missed him, for he'd gone into the house; she stood there waiting for him to emerge, determined to get a good glimpse of him.

He stepped outside and onto his porch, his back to her, his hands on his hips as he surveyed the scene. He was thin, lanky almost, and very tall. His brown hair was floppy and mussed. He wore brown slacks, what appeared to be corduroys, and a gray wool sweater; a red plaid shirt collar peeked from underneath. A dusty-looking gray coat hung from his shoulders and arms. His look was unassuming and conventional, but a little unkempt.

He turned, hands still on hips, and looked around his property. Gwyneth's eyebrows rose: he was younger than he'd looked from behind. He wore thin-rimmed glasses; he adjusted them with a finger where they rested on his nose.

He turned his head upward and appeared to start. Gwyneth gasped aloud and hurried from the window.

GWYNETH FELL INTO A NEW ROUTINE. Whereas before, she'd pull into her driveway after work and hurry into her house to watch the workers from the window, now, she hurried into her house and stared out the window at nothing, waiting for him to appear.

He always did appear, though not always right away. Sometimes he would appear immediately, and she would watch him walk back and forth between the house and the barn, wondering what he was doing. Sometimes she would wait half an hour, only to see him emerge from the barn and stroll into the house, not to reappear. Sometimes she would give up and walk away, leaving her curtain open so she'd more easily see him when he finally came outside.

He received many deliveries. She watched with curiosity as a truckload of boxes was unloaded and brought one by one into the barn. One day, a truck full of wooden boards arrived; another day, what appeared to be a giant cauldron.

He did strange things to his garden. He dug holes in the cold earth, then covered the holes with odd round contraptions. He monitored the plants' progress by measuring their leaves, frequently consulting an old-looking book. Gwyneth was baffled by these unusual behaviors but mostly was intrigued.

Though tall, he had a slight, almost gaunt appearance, his face hollow but pleasing. Gwyneth had noticed he had a habit of pushing his glasses up the bridge of his nose. She wondered if it was a nervous habit, or if he simply had ill-fitting glasses.

Gwyneth frequently heard loud banging and clanking coming from inside the barn. She desperately wanted to know what was going on in there and considered peeking inside when she knew he wasn't at home. She might have, had she not been so worried about being caught: she wasn't afraid she'd get in trouble, but she was terrified of having to talk to him.

Sometimes Tansy joined her at the window. Sometimes Tansy kept her too long at the kitchen table, and Gwyneth longingly glanced at the window, wondering what she was missing.

One night he failed to appear at all. Gwyneth stepped into her bathtub immensely disappointed, and slipped beneath the fragrant water; she soaked for a time, her mind drifting, and reemerged sighing, resolved to going to bed.

On a whim she took one last look out the bathroom window. She was delighted to find that her whim had been rewarded.

She glanced at the clock—it was very nearly midnight. She furrowed her brow, wondering what he was doing this late.

He was in his backyard, planting flowers in the holes he'd covered with domes, painstakingly measuring the rows in perfect lines. He had laid a small blanket where he knelt. His back was to her as he kneeled in the dirt, and his skin glowed in the moonlight. He was naked.

Gwyneth inhaled and opened her eyes wide, stars seeming to twinkle in her blood. She hung back to avoid being seen, peeling the curtain back just enough to peek through. He was standing now, tying what appeared to be a vine to a tall wooden spike. His breath was visible in the air, white ghosts escaping into the frigid Maine night. He'd looked lanky in his clothes, but naked he was lean and muscled, his calves and thighs well-defined, his back and shoulders sinewy and strong. Gwyneth's eyes lingered on his backside, tight, round, and youthful. She watched as his muscles twitched with his movements, admiring unabashedly the mechanisms of his body, which were underlined by the shadows of the night.

Unknowingly under her watchful gaze, he surveyed his work and retrieved his tools from the ground. After replacing them in the shed, he turned and fully faced her; Gwyneth's heart dropped straight to her center. She continued watching as his tall form stalked around the house and up the steps of the porch, then disappeared behind the front door. She climbed into bed, curtains open to the stars, the shadow of his house just creeping up her bed; alone, she twisted and turned in the moonlight, alight with a vision, conspiring with the stars that had seen the vision too.

CHAPTER FOUR

*T*he next day she watched as he pulled into his driveway, practically hidden by the engulfing leaves of some kind of huge, out of control plant. The leaves clung to him like tentacles as he fumbled for the door handle; after struggling to disentangle himself, he nearly fell out of the car, bringing several formidable leaves with him. He rose and dove back inside, emerging sometime later holding it by its roots, which were long, and thick as his thighs. Struggling to maintain a grip, he stumbled with it through the snow toward his garden, his face hidden in its fronds.

He dropped it in a large hole in the center of the garden and brushed the dirt off his coat. He then stood back, surveying his work, and walked with a confident swagger toward his house.

He stopped suddenly, his hands at his sides, and looked right at her through the window. Gwyneth's heart stopped beating. She stepped away and ran from the hallway up the stairs.

AT THE TOP of the stairs Gwyneth paused, her hand on the banister, and closed her eyes. She turned abruptly and pounded halfway down again, then slowed, stopped, and walked evenly back upstairs. After a moment of hesitation she forced herself down again, making it almost to the front door before losing her courage. With a sigh of resignation she went up the stairs for the last time that night, the sting of failure tugging angrily at her gut.

"HI, SUGAR. HOW WAS YOUR DAY?"

"Oh, it was awful. Work lasted forever. I think my boss hates me."

"She doesn't hate you. I thought you loved your job."

"I love my job, not my boss."

"What happened?"

"Well," said Tansy, "I told her she should be looking into coral, not lavender. For the shop. She keeps buying lavender, but that's so last season. Everything I'm reading says coral is going to be big this year."

"That's too bad. Maybe now would be a good time to continue looking at nursing schools."

"Maybe."

A moment or two of silence passed.

"Did you hear back from Ken?" asked Gwyneth.

"Yeah, he said he's been busy or some such nonsense. I think it's a sign that it's over."

"I think it's for the best."

"Me, too," said Tansy. "Especially since there's a new man in my life now."

"Oh?" Gwyneth braced herself for whatever new drama Tansy was about to get into. "Who is it?"

"His name's Brian. He's very handsome, though not as handsome as Van Donnelly, of course. Guess where I met him?"

"Where?"

"He's one of the guys who worked on your neighbor's house!" Tansy laughed. "I gave him my number weeks ago, and he finally got up the nerve to call me. Isn't that fabulous?"

"That's fabulous, sugar. Have a good time."

Tansy's voice became softer. "Are you okay, Ma? You sound sad, for some reason."

Inexplicably, Gwyneth began crying. "I'm not sad." She rubbed her eyes with her hand, then stared at her wet fingers in amazement. *What in hell is this?*

"Do you want to talk about it?"

"There's nothing to talk about."

Tansy said nothing, and a few moments passed in silence.

"Do you want to come over for some tea?" asked Gwyneth.

"Sure," said Tansy instantly. "Just give me five minutes."

CHAPTER FIVE

*O*ver the next week, Gwyneth did not need to work hard to watch him, because he was outside every night, promptly at midnight, and to Gwyneth's disappointment he was clothed without fail. However, her eyes had retained the image of him, and somehow his bland, ill-fitting clothing made the knowledge of his secret litheness all the more interesting.

When she returned home from work he always had a large delivery waiting at his new shed's door, sometimes columns of boxes, and sometimes flats of new plants. Sometimes he'd open them before bringing them inside, having spotted them from his car as he pulled into the driveway and run to see what they were. Gwyneth was continuously perplexed by the contents of these boxes. Sometimes they were jars—hundreds, it seemed, of jars. Sometimes they were strings of lights. Sometimes ribbons. Sometimes books.

Then finally one night, a few minutes after midnight, she heard a voice. She sat up straight in her bathtub, her long hair sticking to her body in graying red clumps. Rising, she peered through the window, surprised to find it was snowing. She gazed in reverence at the sky a moment before her attention was drawn downward toward motion on the ground. It was then that she spotted his naked shivering form moving before the garden.

She frantically emerged from the tub and donned her bathrobe, then knelt on the floor by the window to watch.

His back was to her; his hands were outstretched. He was standing straight and firm among the steady snowfall, as if preaching to the snow-covered flowers, and his chin was lifted high toward the sky. Gwyneth gathered her courage and opened the window a crack. From the distance, she heard him speaking; though she couldn't hear his words, she recognized the soft, even cadence of poetry.

In the blackness of the night and with winter's first snowfall around him, the universe silent but for his steady rhythm and rhymes, he appeared to be summoning magic, willing the flowers to rise through his soul. The snowflakes drifted like stardust, a choir of witnesses illuminating the night before vanishing into the earth.

Watching from above, Gwyneth felt the vulnerability of humankind, how small we appear to the universe, how defenseless we are against its elements. But in our smallness, it seemed, we are not powerless; we can summon storms and pull flowers from the snow. Despite the frozen air seeping in from the window, Gwyneth felt warm with enchantment.

His recitations ceased, and he lowered his hands. Then he hunched in the cold and hastened through the snow into the warm safety of his house.

~

THE UPCOMING WEEK WAS THANKSGIVING. It was one of the only times Gwyneth regretted not having any family, and that wasn't for her own sake but rather for Tansy's. Gwyneth had always wished Tansy had had grandparents, cousins, aunts and uncles, people to play with, people to love. Her parents had passed away years ago, and she didn't have any siblings.

The good news was that Tansy always seemed happy to have Thanksgiving at Gwyneth's house. She usually invited a few girl-friends. It was a warm, cozy, comfortable holiday.

Gwyneth decorated her house with fall flowers and scented candles. When Tansy arrived, two friends in tow, she admired the scene with enthusiasm, filling the rooms with her usual blustery cheer.

"This is your best year yet," she told her as she stood by the sideboard making cocktails. She handed Gwyneth a martini glass. "Want one?"

"Yes," said Gwyneth, taking the glass and hugging her daughter with her other arm. "And thank you."

It had occurred to Gwyneth that perhaps her neighbor, who'd moved all alone to this secluded Maine town, would need somewhere to go for the holiday. However, the day before Thanksgiving, Gwyneth observed him throwing an overnight bag in his car and driving away. As he did not return that night or the next morning, she assumed he'd had somewhere to go after all.

A couple of days after Thanksgiving, Gwyneth sat at her work desk gazing out into the snowy landscape. Leona was at a meeting, and the Historical Society building was quiet. Though she liked her boss and enjoyed the erratic nature of days when they worked together, she relished the solitude, especially in winter. The peace meant she was ahead on her work, and she was thinking of the snowfall last night when the bell tinkling over the door aroused her from her thoughts.

She directed her attention toward the front of the building, prepared to greet her visitor. Her heart began racing as her eyes fell on her neighbor, whose face was lifted in awe toward the high ceilings and intricately carved beams. After a moment or two, his gaze fell downward. He started with shock when he saw her at her desk.

"Oh," he muttered, and pushed his glasses up the bridge of his nose. "I'm sorry, you scared me. I mean, you didn't scare me, per se. You startled me." He cleared his throat and pushed his glasses up again. "What I mean is," he said, appearing to deliberately slow down, "that I think you are my neighbor."

"I am," Gwyneth squeaked, and closed her eyes a moment against the vision of him naked in the snow. Once recovered, she smiled sweetly and rose to meet him. Approaching, she clasped her hands before her waist, noting he was taller than he appeared from afar. "It's a pleasure to meet you. My name is Gwyneth O'Shaughnessy."

"Gwyneth O'Shaughnessy," he repeated, eyebrows raised. "That's the most beautiful name I've ever heard, like something out of an ancient poem."

"Oh," she said, blushing. "That's a very nice thing to say. And your name is Liam Baxter." She added quickly, "My boss told me."

"Oh. Of course, of course." He shifted where he stood and pushed up his glasses once more. "This being the Historical Society, and all."

"Yes. Your house sat empty for many years. We were all very excited when we learned it would be renovated."

"Oh. Yes, yes. I'm sure, I'm sure." He looked around the room again, then met her eyes with a smile. "It's a very special house. It deserves to be brought back to life." A conspiratorial twinkle reached his eyes; up close, Gwyneth saw that they were an earthy hazel, round and wide. "I think of the house as an old man getting a brand new haircut and wardrobe." He chuckled. "A lot of people think I'm pretty peculiar."

He had a clear, silvery voice, and the creases in his forehead suggested someone perpetually thinking. *How old is he?* she wondered. *I put him mid-thirties, perhaps.* Despite his awkwardness, he was undeniably charming, and Gwyneth watched him with delight. "Well, not me. And not Leona. If you want to anthropomorphize a house, this is the place to do it."

"Good to know." He pushed his glasses up the bridge of his nose. "Good to know, indeed."

Some seconds of silence passed, and Gwyneth cleared her throat to fill it.

"Did you need some help with something?"

"Oh. Oh yes, of course. I was curious to know more about my house. The history, and all."

"Sure. You can look through our records over here."

Gwyneth led him through a doorway into a little side room lined with bookshelves. She searched the spines and pulled an old black tome off the shelf, then placed it on a table for him to look through.

"This outlines the buildings of the town by street," she said, flipping delicately through the yellowing pages. She stopped halfway through and pointed. "Here's my house," she said. "And here's the history of yours."

"Wow." His face was soft with awe as he bent forward to look at the fading ink, his face scrunched with interest. After a few moments of reverential silence, he adjusted his glasses and stood straight. "This is magnificent. Thank you."

She smiled at him, and he smiled back, brightly. *How expressive his eyes are*, thought Gwyneth, intrigued.

"So what brings you to Dearham, Maine?" she asked. "Leona says you're from Boston."

"Oh. Oh yes. I liked it well enough, until I got divorced. I felt like I needed a change. So I sold my townhouse and moved to the country. I like it here." He stuck his hands in his pockets and looked about. "I wasn't sure I would, to be honest. But the country suits me just fine."

Gwyneth was curious about his divorce, and her own tender heart ached to imagine him in pain. Not wishing to pry, she merely smiled kindly. "What will you be doing out here? You quit your job, I presume."

He seemed to stiffen a little. "Well," he began, his finger nudging up his glasses, "I'm using this time as a sabbatical of sorts. I've been exploring the Maine countryside, mostly, and learning about my new home. I'm opening up my own business here, but"—he swallowed, seeming to choose his words—"the timing hasn't been right. The timing is right now, so I'll be home more."

"The timing?"

"Say," he said, walking toward an antique map on the wall, "can we talk about that later?" He pointed to a spot on the map. "This is us. Isn't it?"

Gwyneth stepped toward the map and followed the line of his finger. "Yes, that's Dearham. This is Yardley Reach, right here."

"The causeway. Of course, of course. I take it every day as I go in and out of town. What's the history of that causeway?"

"The causeway was built in 1904 with the increase in the popularity of automobiles, when people began feeling dissatisfied with the ferry service. It was reconstructed in 1953 in an effort to provide jobs after the war—that's when they added the beautiful iron guard rails."

"The guard rails." Liam's face brightened, revealing plentiful laugh lines, and Gwyneth's face brightened in response. "I noticed they're similar to the original fence around my front yard. I don't suppose there's a correlation?"

"There is," said Gwyneth happily; it was delightful to talk to someone who appreciated these details, and Liam was very easy to talk to. "The Mullany brothers were ship owners who owned an ironworks. Their primary business was granite, but they dabbled in everything. They practically owned this town in the nineteenth century, and signs of them are everywhere. Their trademark rosette is in the iron guard rails on the causeway, as well as on the stakes of your fence."

"Aha!"

Gwyneth's eyes widened, and she straightened.

Liam cleared his throat and pushed his glasses up the bridge of his nose. "Excuse me, I get a little excited." He attempted a smile. "You see, I'm starting a business, and I've been trying to design a logo. I wonder if I could incorporate that rosette, somehow. Not exactly, of course. A subtle nod, perhaps?"

"What a nice idea."

Gwyneth yearned desperately to ask him about his business; however, as he offered no more information, she said nothing.

"Well," he said, gesturing toward the table. "Thank you for directing me to these books. I shouldn't keep you."

"Oh. It's no trouble." She backed away, out through the doorway and toward her desk, where she turned to her laptop and attempted to write her newsletter. From the other room, out of sight, came the sounds of books being moved and pages being flipped through—cozy, homey sounds, the kinds that provide comfort on brisk winter days.

LIAM VISITED AGAIN the next day: he wanted to know more about the Mullany brothers.

"Leona wrote a biography of them. She had a few dozen printed for those of us interested in the history. There's a copy on the bookshelf." Gwyneth withdrew from the shelf a thick tome with a simple white cover, a sepia-toned photo square in the middle. Liam took it from her outstretched hand and held it reverentially in both of his. "You can find their original letters right here," she told him, gingerly removing a book with preserved nineteenth-century letters, yellowed with age.

Liam murmured with interest, studying the elaborate, loopy handwriting.

"I've transcribed the letters," she said, smiling a little with pride. "There's a database on the computer, if the letters are too difficult to read."

"Oh, it's not too difficult. The handwriting is a pleasure. I enjoy the voyage back in time." He straightened, suddenly looking quite serious. "No disrespect to your transcription, of course."

"None taken at all." He didn't need anything more from her, yet she was reluctant to leave. She took a chance. "I could tell you a little about their lives, if you'd like."

Liam's face lit up. "Please do." He gestured toward the table, and they both sat down.

Encouraged, Gwyneth sat. She picked Leona's biography from off the table and turned to the middle, which offered a few dozen illustrations and photographs.

"This is Mr. Richard Mullany," she explained, pointing. "He owned the granite quarry on the edge of town."

Liam regarded the photograph studiously. The man in the photo was slim and upright, with a lush dark handlebar mustache and thick mutton chop sideburns. Though his face was rigid, as was typical in his day, there was a smile in his eyes, making them seem to sparkle with latent good humor.

Gwyneth snuck a glance at Liam. He, too, possessed a face of good humor—not rigid, like Mr. Mullany's, but thoughtful, intellectual—in a loose, unfettered way.

His eyes met hers, and she flushed. She started and cleared her throat, then directed her attention to the book once more.

"This is his brother, Mr. Hubert Mullany. Hubert was an investor, an inventor, an artist—more of a Renaissance man. He owned ships that used to transport Richard's granite, among other things. There's an interesting story about him. The story goes that he was unlucky in love. The woman he loved, Angelina Tunis, promised him for years she would consider accepting his hand. Eventually she married another man. When her husband died of consumption, he renewed his courtship, but to no avail. In a gesture of closure, he renamed his ship—it had been called

The Angelina. Once renamed, it sank, and with it, its entire crew."

Liam's eyes were wide as he listened. "What happened to Hubert?"

"He died an old bachelor."

Liam nodded thoughtfully, then smiled. "Well. I suppose he preferred to be alone than with someone who wasn't right for him."

"Yes." Gwyneth looked away, toward the window. "I can understand that," she muttered.

"I can, too."

Gwyneth looked at him. She shouldn't ask, but curiosity got the best of her.

"You can?"

"Sure." He pushed his glasses up. "I was married, but I'm not anymore."

"I know you mentioned you were divorced."

"Yes." Liam arranged the papers on the desk neatly until it was impossible to tell there was more than one; he then lined the bottom of the stack so it was perfectly parallel to the edge of the table. "The divorce," he said. "I haven't been with anyone since the divorce. For that reason."

"I haven't dated a lot, either," said Gwyneth, tentatively; she wasn't used to talking about herself, especially not about such a personal topic, but opening up to him was somehow thrilling. "My daughter thinks I should."

"You have a daughter?"

"Yes. She's grown, though. In her twenties."

"Are you close with her?"

"Very."

"That's nice." Liam smiled kindly. "I don't have any children. I wouldn't mind children, but I would be content without them."

"Did your wife want children?"

"No. She was very career oriented. It was understood before

we got married." He straightened a couple of pens until they were aligned just so. "Do you have just the one daughter, then?"

"Just the one, yes. I had her so very young. I might have had others, I suppose, but I never found the right person." Gwyneth paused to delight in this intimate conversation. She couldn't remember the last time someone had confided in her, aside from Tansy—whom she loved with all her heart, and more. Still, it had been a long time since Gwyneth had had someone to talk to who was not dependent on her, to whom she wasn't a mentor; it had been a long time since she'd had—well, a friend. Could Liam become her friend? It was silly to be so presumptuous, she supposed. Gwyneth had forgotten how lovely it was to converse with someone...not her own age, surely. How old was Liam, anyhow?

"How old are you?" she asked.

He cleared his throat, pushed his glasses up, and smiled. "Well, I'm thirty-five."

"I'm forty-seven."

"A twelve-year difference," he noted, evidently with great interest: his brow had risen and creased, and his smile grew even wider. "Now, that's serendipitous."

Lord, is he not full of mysteries. "Why?"

He pushed his glasses up, then folded and refolded his hands as they rested on the table. "I'm reading this book. Of poetry, you see. And twelve is a very important number."

"Oh? Is it related to the numbers on the clock?"

"No, it's the number of goddesses and the number of realms within their dominions."

"Oh."

Liam's face flushed. They stared at each other in silence.

"I, um," he said finally, with an awkward laugh and a push of his eyeglasses. "I don't necessarily believe in them. It's interesting reading." He shrugged.

Gwyneth had a vision of him standing naked in his garden, his hands outstretched toward the snow.

"I saw you," she said.

His forehead turned downward with confusion. "You saw me where?"

Gwyneth wasn't sure what had prompted her to be so bold, but boldness felt titillating. "In your garden. Reciting your poetry. I saw you."

Liam stared at her: the flush that had crept into his face now drained until it was white.

"Ah," he said, pushing his glasses up. "So."

Gwyneth hesitated. "Can I ask you something?"

"First," he said, shifting in his seat, "please allow me to apologize. I had no idea anyone was watching. If I had—"

"It's okay," she told him, and ventured to pat his hand. "No apologies necessary."

He didn't respond to this, but looked at her with warm, grateful eyes. "As to your question. It's rather hard to explain. I should say, it isn't hard to explain, but I fear the explanation will make you think I'm a little strange."

"My dear Liam, I've seen you gardening naked in the middle of the night, in the snow. I already think you're strange."

They both laughed at this. The mood relaxed.

The sound of the bell on the front door made them both turn. Gwyneth's face fell.

"I'm guessing you need to tend to that," said Liam.

"Yes." Gwyneth stood and straightened her skirt. "We'll have to finish this conversation later."

"Of course, of course."

Gwyneth hesitated before walking away. "We could..." Her heart dropped to her feet; she attempted a casual smile. "We could continue tonight, if you'd like. You could...You could come over for dinner."

"Oh." Liam's eyes brightened, and he pushed his glasses up the bridge of his nose. He smiled, bringing out the smile lines in his face. "Why, thank you, Gwyneth. I'd very much enjoy that."

"Great." Gwyneth with effort held back her excitement; she inhaled deeply and grinned at him. "I'll be home at five-thirty. Come over at six-thirty."

"Okay." Liam nodded with decision. "Six-thirty it is."

Gwyneth's smile turned more serious. She waved, turned, and glided to the doorway to meet her visitor, conscious of his gaze, the flutter of anticipation in her breast.

CHAPTER SIX

That afternoon Gwyneth pulled too quickly into her driveway and climbed out at once, closing the door with a hasty shove and making her way toward her house. Clasped in her hands were the canvas grocery bags she kept in the trunk of her car, currently filled with cheese, bread, cream, various herbs, and two small pumpkins. It was a day when snowflakes drift breezily from the trees, when the silence sits in the air with patient expectation. She tramped her way through the snow, which collected around her boots and along the bottom of her skirt.

Entering her house, she pulled off her boots and coat, leaving on her scarf as she made her way with her grocery bags to her farmhouse-style kitchen. She unloaded the ingredients onto the butcher block countertop and began cutting into her pumpkins, which she then cleaned out and stuffed with chopped bread, cheese, and herbs. She placed them on a baking sheet and stuck them in the oven, then sat at the kitchen table to read, though she was unable to retain much of what she was reading, and her foot kept kicking of its own accord as she anxiously fiddled with her hair. After a time, the doorbell rang, making her jump. She straightened a few stray wisps of hair around her face in the hallway mirror, then approached the door and peered through the peephole. She swung the door open slowly, smiling when she saw the innocent curiosity in his face.

"Hello, Liam," said Gwyneth. She looked him over: he was wearing brown corduroy pants, a wool sweater, and a plaid collared shirt beneath. Lean and lanky from afar, his form appeared stronger, more substantial, up close. She was happy to see him, happy for the masculine company. She smiled sweetly as their eyes met. "Come on in. No coat?" She closed the door as he stepped inside and brushed his feet on the floor to force off the snow.

"Ah, it's just next door," he said. "The cold doesn't bother me too much."

I know, said Gwyneth to herself.

An awkward silence passed. She met his eyes, and he blushed.

He cleared his throat and extended his hand, which was clasping a bottle of wine. "I brought this for you. For us."

"Oh. Thank you." Gwyneth took the wine and looked at the label. "*Tansy Fields Vineyard.*" She looked up at him with wide eyes. "How did you know?"

"How did I know what?"

"About Tansy."

"Tansy?"

"Tansy is my daughter." She began walking toward the kitchen, and he followed a couple of steps behind. She paused momentarily by a picture frame hanging on the wall. "That's her, right there."

"Ah." Liam peered at the photo, studying it. "I see some resemblance."

"Most people say we look nothing alike."

"Does she look more like..." he began, but trailed off.

"Does she look more like her father? She looks just like him.

36

She has the shape of his face, and his full lips. But she has my eyes." Gwyneth pointed, extending a delicate slender finger.

"Yes." Liam leaned in and squinted. "Yes, I think she does." He stood back and regarded the other pictures. "Is this her father?" he asked gently, pointing. "Right here?"

"Yes." Gwyneth looked at the picture of herself with the handsome dark-haired man her daughter revered without ever having met.

Liam was studying the picture. "He looks like Van Donnelly."

"Tansy says that all the time."

"Truthfully, I think she resembles you more."

"Tansy is beautiful, so I won't argue."

They stood back and faced each other. Gwyneth rubbed her hands together nervously, then cleared her throat and smiled. "Tansy lives right over in Bar Harbor," she said, making her way to the kitchen once more; the fire cracked in the hearth, a cozy, comforting sound. "She manages The Salty Seashell gift shop. She might even pop in—sometimes she comes over after work."

"That must be nice for you." Liam smiled. Then he inhaled deeply, and his eyes brightened. "That smells sensational."

"Thanks." With a *pop*, Gwyneth removed the cork from the wine bottle and poured into two stemless glasses. "It's one of my favorite recipes. It's called 'pumpkin stuffed with everything good.'"

"That sounds intriguing, and delicious. What's in it?"

"Crusty bread, gruyere cheese, thyme, nutmeg—and a few other things."

"That really is everything good."

He took the glass she offered and clinked it with hers.

"Cheers," he said.

"Cheers."

They sipped their wine and smiled at each other.

"Do you have other family nearby?" he asked.

"No. My parents passed away years ago, but"—she hesitated a moment, and swallowed—"we weren't close."

"I'm in the opposite situation. My family's all in Boston. There are a lot of them. I love them, but I don't mind putting a few miles between us, truth be told."

"Don't you get along?"

"Sure, sure. We get along just fine. Sometimes close quarters can crush you, though. You know?"

Gwyneth's timer went off. She slipped on her oven mitts and slid the baking tray from the oven.

Two stuffed pumpkins, touched with golden brown, released their earthy fragrances as the warmth from the oven wafted through the kitchen. Within the pumpkins, cheese and cream bubbled around chunks of bread and herbs. Gwyneth paused a moment to savor the scents, then with two wooden spoons lifted them onto two plates. She took the plates in her hands and turned.

"Dinner is served."

"Holy moly." His eyebrows rose above the rims of his glasses. He had a look of perpetual curiosity that gave him the appearance of a mischievous little boy. "How did you do that?"

Gwyneth chuckled. "It isn't that hard. All I did was follow a recipe."

He gently took the plates from her hands and nodded toward the dining room. "And now, I'll follow you."

They moved into the dining room, where a big farm table rested heavily on a wide-planked floor.

"It's a little drafty in here," said Gwyneth, tightening her scarf as she sat. "I'm sorry."

"What an absolutely delightful room." Liam looked about: a forged metal canopy chandelier offered scant light, and the flickering candlesticks Gwyneth had placed on the table cast dancing shadows on the plaster walls. He turned his attention to Gwyneth and smiled. "I love old houses, as you know."

"Did you live in an old house in Boston?"

"In Boston? Yes. Yes, I did." As he spoke, he straightened his plate and silverware so they were arranged perfectly in a neat, satisfying line. "Maura and I had a brownstone in Back Bay. It was beautiful, just gorgeous."

"But you didn't like the city?"

"Boston's a great city filled with history and culture. You never lack something interesting to do. Like all cities, it can be over-whelming. That being said, it's easy to blend in there, if you want to."

"And you wanted to?"

"I...well, I suppose I did. I was an investment banker, and I did pretty well, if you don't mind my saying. I enjoyed my work, but after the divorce, I needed a break."

"A break from what?"

"From...everything, I guess. From pressure."

"I suppose your career was very stressful."

"Yes, but I didn't really mind it. I mean personally, though. I have my...eccentricities, you see. At least, that's what Maura called them. It...it was hard...to try to be someone I'm not."

Gwyneth wanted to know more, but he seemed content to stop there.

"It is hard," she said, "when you feel your life isn't all you thought it would be."

"I guess I just want my life to be more meaningful. I...was a little depressed during the divorce. If I'm honest. I had a little bit of a breakdown. It made me reevaluate what I was doing with my life."

"That's understandable."

Neither said anything for a moment or two.

"Now that I'm here," he said, "I'd like to do some charity work, maybe. I spent so much time making money for people who already had so much of it. Maybe I can help raise up some people who need it."

"What a lovely idea. I think that will be very satisfying."

"I think so. Plus, it would make me feel part of my new town." He paused. "You know," he said, with a little chuckle, "it's really rather ironic. How you can be equally alone in the city, among millions, or in the country, among only a few."

"Do you want to be alone?"

Liam said nothing for a moment or two. "Well," he said, pushing up his glasses, "every day changes, now, doesn't it?"

Gwyneth pondered these words. She sipped her wine, then picked up the bottle and looked again at the label. "What a coincidence that you brought me this bottle." She regarded the whimsical illustration of fairies floating above a bouquet of yellow tansy buttons. "And such a pretty picture, too."

"I just liked the name. I don't really know that much about wine. I'm one of those people who buys the wine by the label."

"I do that, too. And I love the name Tansy. I chose it for my daughter because it means eternal life."

"It's also a flowering herb. That's what drew me to the label."

They gingerly dug into their pumpkins' steaming centers. Gwyneth pulled out a hearty chunk of bread, cheese, and herbs, blew on it, then carefully placed it in her mouth. Her lips closed around her fork, and she sighed internally at its deep, lusty flavors.

Liam, mouth full, moaned aloud. He chewed slowly and swallowed, then quickly dug in for more. "This is phenomenal. The best thing I've ever tasted."

"Thank you." Gwyneth blushed and shifted in her chair, the wine beginning to warm her insides and tickle her blood. "I'm so glad you like it."

"Are you a self-taught cook?"

"Yes. I was a single mother at a very young age. I had to figure it out myself, or my daughter didn't eat. I didn't have anyone to teach me."

"Do you mind..." he began, and stopped to swallow. "Do you mind...if I ask..."

"He passed away." Gwyneth said the words automatically. Secrets flittered through her mind like papers tossed up into the air; she didn't know how much to tell him. "My daughter never met her father. She's twenty-eight. Closer to you in age than I am." She laughed once, awkwardly.

Liam watched her, his eyes gentle, waiting patiently for her to continue.

Gwyneth cleared her throat and looked into his earthy eyes. "Her father—" Suddenly, she changed her mind, settling on vague. "There are some things about her father she doesn't know. I've—" She bit her lip. "I've not told her the whole story."

Liam was silent a moment, making sure she was through. "Well, Gwyneth," he said softly; he wasn't smiling, but the lines in his face suggested a smile. "I have no doubt you've had good reason."

Gwyneth wondered. "Have I?" she asked, her voice high, a little frantic. She calmed herself, looked about the room, then directed her attention to his face once more. She found it warm and sympathetic, his eyes wide and intent. "What's a good reason to one can be selfish to another."

"We all do the best we can."

She said no more on the subject, and mercifully, he didn't press her. They ate their dinner, chatting over wine. Gwyneth resisted the desire to ask him about the poetry and the gardening. As they discussed all manner of subjects—the Maine weather, her work at the historical society, world events—the question was a presence, always hovering over her tongue.

After dinner, she served dessert—a winter fruit salad with homemade whipped cream. Gwyneth felt satisfied in body and mind, and she indulged in a deep, relaxing breath, relishing the scents of coffee and firewood. Their conversation flowed freely, and Gwyneth was feeling lulled by the full-bodied wine.

The grandfather clock struck eleven, and they both glanced upward with surprise.

"Oh, dear," said Liam. "Have I really been here that long?"

Gwyneth frowned as he stood to leave, and stood herself, but slowly. "You're not leaving, are you?"

He said nothing a moment, then raised his eyebrows inquiringly. "Would you prefer for me to stay?"

"No. I mean, yes. I mean..." She twiddled her fingers nervously, not wanting to give him the wrong impression. "What I mean is, you haven't even finished your story yet."

"My story?"

"Yes. The story about your poetry. About your garden." She offered a coy little smile. "You promised me you would."

"Oh!" He slapped his forehead and nodded. "Yes. Yes, indeed I did. Well, I..." He studied her thoughtfully, until a grin touched the corners of his lips. "Well, I could just show you."

"Oh." Gwyneth's brow rose with intrigue. "Oh, all right."

Gwyneth put on her coat. They stepped into their boots and headed outside into the darkness.

The snow was newly fallen, the last remnants drifting softly from the trees. Despite the frozen ground, the night felt warm like the hours after snowfall always do, and somehow to Gwyneth Liam's nighttime excursions were no longer as perplexing.

At the door to the barn, Liam stopped.

"I just need to grab something," he said.

He stuck his key in the lock and pushed the door open enough to allow him to grab his coat from a hook and an item from a shadowy corner. When he reemerged, Gwyneth saw that the item was a book.

After slipping into his coat, he held the book in the air to show her. "Over here," he said, nodding toward the garden.

Gwyneth followed, trailing a step or two behind, as he strolled across the snow. Gwyneth observed her house from this new angle; she hadn't realized how old it looked. Together, they walked into his garden, which at this close distance proved to be laid in straight, neat rows.

Gwyneth looked about. It was perfectly symmetrical, lined with some sort of scraggly gray-leafed herbs. Each of the four quadrants housed three different plants. In the center was the big ugly plant that had nearly swallowed him in his car.

Gwyneth pointed before she thought about it. "That plant is growing nicely here."

Liam stared at her. "Yes."

Gwyneth blushed. "I noticed...you know." She swallowed. "I couldn't help but notice."

Liam and Gwyneth exchanged a long look. Neither said anything. Gwyneth coughed nervously.

"So," she croaked, and cleared her throat. "What is the plant, exactly?"

"Ah," he said, straightening, and directing his attention to the garden. "That"—he pointed—"is Aedrian's Star."

"I've never heard of that. Where did it come from?"

Liam scratched his head. "Ah. Well, I grew it."

"But I saw you driving home with it in your car," countered Gwyneth, her curiosity greater than her concern at being discovered spying on him from her window.

"I grew it someplace else." Liam shifted and smiled awkwardly. "The conditions here...weren't quite right."

Gwyneth looked at him quizzically. "But what do you mean?"

Liam drew attention to the book in his hands: he held it in front of her face for her to read.

"*Goddess in the Garden: Llewellyn's Poetic Energy as Resurrected in the Harvest of Moriander*," read Gwyneth. She read it again, silently, her lips moving over the cryptic phrases. She turned her face upward toward his, and waited, stumped.

"It's a lost mythology," he said quietly. "Of unknown origin. Open it."

Gwyneth took the book from his hands; it was an old book with a deep blue cover, its title relayed in ornate gold script. The gossamer pages seemed frail as spiderwebs as they drifted between her fingers; Gwyneth feared they'd disintegrate at her touch. She turned to the page saved with a faded ribbon. On the left was a whimsical sketch of a figure dancing among tall plants under a full moon. On the right was the following poem:

> *To please Moriander, Aedrian's Star*
> *Is raised in water, twelve halos far.*
>
> *By rock She grows until She's wise;*
> *She migrates under full moon's rise.*
>
> *Do listen, now, and be aware,*
> *For Moriander's desires I shall share.*
>
> *The Star shall come to final rest*
> *The center of Her Garden's breast.*
>
> *Her fertile bed is in the ground,*
> *Three starwidths long, three widths around.*
>
> *East, West, South and North*
> *Yira's Birds shall offer forth*
>
> *While cradling Namis blooms, twelve wide,*
> *With twelve Rose Hearts like rings inside.*
>
> *Like planets will Her fronds begin*
> *To lull in orbit her moons therein*

When brought to rest in brightest Heaven,
At midnight harvest, month Eleven.

Gwyneth read the poem again, but the words twirled and turned in on themselves; she couldn't parse their meaning.

He gently reclaimed the book, but held it for her to see, and pointed as he read.

"Aedrian's Star," he said. "It's raised in water, twelve halos far."

"What's a halo?"

"A halo is a unit of measurement. It's about the equivalent of a mile and a half. That's where I grew her. It," he corrected quickly. "That's where I grew it."

"But..." Gwyneth was full of questions. She looked to the garden, buying time to think, then back at him. "But where did you find Aedrian's Star here in Maine?"

"I came across the bulb almost by accident, a while back, when I was exploring. A woman sold it to me, and I grew the Star right here. 'By rock She grows until she's wise.' I grew her out at Pierce's Cove, the rocky beach off Route 34."

Gwyneth's mind was swimming. She was silent, utterly at a loss.

Liam was pointing into his garden. "Three starwidths," he said. "That's a unit of measurement, too. About six feet long, it is. These next bits tell you what should go in each quadrant, and in what order. The Star, it says, will help grow them. As long as you harvest them at midnight. Month Eleven. That's November."

"But why?"

Liam studied her for a moment, then looked out toward his garden.

"I know it must seem pretty bizarre," he said, and he sighed, his face long and thoughtful. "I don't really understand it myself. At least, not fully. I don't believe in any of this, you know." He closed the book and stared at it, then met her eyes once more. He smiled forlornly. "I shouldn't be saying that out loud, I suppose."

Gwyneth waited and watched him in the silvery moonlight. His eyes were deep as the earth.

"I've always loved mythology, you see. I love to draw gods, heroes, mythical creatures, etcetera. I always have, ever since I was a boy. I left my drawings all over our house in Boston. They used to irritate Maura. She thought they were weird."

A light gust of wind shook the trees, scattering snowflakes, which danced about them like fairies. Gwyneth was intrigued by the softness of his voice, the unintended sorrow that laced his every word.

"So this book," he went on, flipping through its pages. "I found it lying in the street. I was walking home from signing the divorce papers. I didn't know what to do or where to go. And it was lying there, literally, in the middle of the street. How serendipitous is that?"

Gwyneth had sensed a deep-rooted sadness in him; there was something about his eyes, bright with life, but with the shadow of disillusionment. Perhaps that explained her interest in him; curiosity had not served her well in the past. She smiled at his sincerity, waiting for him go on.

"I picked it up and took it home, but it was weeks before I opened it. One day I noticed it sitting on my bookshelf. I thought, 'If I don't read that book, it's likely no one ever will again.' I didn't like that. It seemed unfair. I opened it and read one of the poems. When I was done, I read another one. I felt like I was saving them...from obscurity, from death. It was as if..." He paused and swallowed. "It was as if they lived through me. Someone's words. Someone who had died, and now was alive again, because of me." He laughed nervously. "I'll bet that sounds ridiculous."

"No," said Gwyneth, looking about her at the snow, the sky, Aedrian's Star and her moons in orbit. "I think it's beautiful." In fact, she was entranced. The silence of the night was eloquent as any music; it surrounded and embraced them, hovering in the garden like magic.

"Anyway." Liam regarded the book in his hands. "I feel connected somehow to this mythology. I think my fascination stems less from the content itself and more from the power of the human mind that created it. The idea that there's a system, a universe, that someone else can see. I like that. I've often felt that way myself."

"Who is that someone? Where does the mythology come from?"

"*Goddess in the Garden* was written by someone named Llewellyn. I don't know the first name; the book doesn't say. I don't even know if Llewellyn is a man or a woman." He paused and looked at her; one corner of his mouth ticked upward. "I personally believe she's a woman."

"Me too," Gwyneth agreed, giddily, and the two shared a conspiratorial silent moment.

Liam said, "Llewellyn quotes passages from the mythology of Moriander, who appears to be some kind of Earth goddess who draws her strength from flowers. But she doesn't drain the flowers, you see. She enhances them by imbuing them with her power."

"I like that idea."

"I like it, too. Llewellyn lays it all out in her poems. She tells you just how to plant your garden, where to plant the seeds, and how to harvest them."

"And your chanting outside naked in the middle of a snowy night?"

"Here." Liam flipped through the book until he found the page, then handed the book back to Gwyneth, who read:

> *When Aedrian's tendrils sprawl in Earth,*
> *'Tis time for Moriander's birth.*

Unfettered as a babe just born,
The hour night does shift to morn,

In solitary sacred stealth
Betwixt eleventh day, and twelfth

Recite aloud Her hymnal thrice
Her healing blooms to thus entice;

Your words shall bring the cleansing snow
Through which her tender blossoms grow.

"How odd," said Gwyneth, almost more to herself than to him. "It was snowing that night. It's almost as if..."

"It's almost as if it worked," he finished for her, and his sly smile returned. "Weird, right? Considering it isn't even true."

"Mmm." Gwyneth looked at the garden and its snow-dusted flowers waiting to bloom. She remembered watching him that night, naked in the snow, arms lifted, as if summoning the snowflakes that fell to the earth around him. "It isn't so weird. You do it with passion. If you feel it in your heart, there's at least some truth to it." She looked at him and smiled. "The poems. They're all about creating your own universe. And that's what you've done here, you know."

He smiled gratefully, his kind features even softer in the soft silvery moonlight. "Thank you, Gwyneth," he said, pushing his glasses up with his fingertips. "I really do appreciate that."

She indicated his glasses with a quick upward flick of her finger. "You didn't do that at all, you know. Just now. You didn't push your glasses up the entire time you were talking about this."

He stared at her mutely for a moment or two. "Oh. Right."

"I hope you don't mind my saying that. I don't mean to embarrass you."

"Oh, no, no. Right. No, you didn't embarrass me. You're right, of course. What do you think it means? Shall we psychoanalyze it?"

"Well, I don't think it's all that mysterious. I think it means you're more comfortable in that world."

"Yes."

Gwyneth began to shiver; the cold was creeping into her bones. She wrapped her arms around herself and squeezed.

"I think..." he began, "if you don't mind my saying, that maybe I'm also comfortable with you."

Gwyneth looked up. He wasn't smiling, but the lines in his face suggested one was latent in his words.

"Can you keep a secret?" he said.

Gwyneth's blood raced feverishly. She nodded.

"Do you want to see the coolest part?"

"Yes."

"Okay, then," he said, his eyes wide with excitement. "Check this out."

He led her back toward the barn, where he pushed the door open and flipped on a light switch. They stepped inside. What Gwyneth saw then made her gasp out loud.

"Oh!" she cried, her hands at her chest, turning around to look here and there, barely able to believe her own eyes. "Oh, it's so beautiful!"

"Do you think so?" he asked, but she barely heard: all around her were strings of white fairy lights—dipping from the ceiling in bulbous half moons, draped across doorways in lazy arches, dropping down walls in elegant cascades. The effect was magnificent, ethereal and sublime. Gwyneth shook her head in disbelief.

"It's exquisite," she breathed, looking upward at the high peaked ceiling with exposed wooden beams. Lights were hanging from the beams like chandelier candles, like teardrops, like stars. "How did you do this? *Why* did you do this? What on Earth is all of this for?"

"Are you ready for this?" He took a deep breath. "It's for my jam."

Gwyneth blinked. "Your what?"

"My jam. Look. Look here." He directed her toward the front wall of the barn, where a door led to an alcove she hadn't known existed. In the alcove was a long stove with multiple burners. At her feet were several dozen boxes. Liam bent and flipped one open: inside were rows and rows of jars.

"It's a kitchen." Gwyneth's eyes darted about the room, taking in the oversized pots and pans—and the cauldron she'd seen him receive weeks before. She looked to him to explain; she was speechless.

"Yes. This is where I'll make my jam. I have shelves to display in the store"—he pointed toward the room from where they'd just emerged—"and a register that has to be installed. That should be delivered this week."

"But where will the jam come from?"

"From my garden," he replied, as if it were the most obvious thing in the world. "Rootberry, roseberry, angel herb, and sugarwood—that's just to start. Llewellyn's poems are most specific about those, so there won't be as much guesswork. I'd like to dabble in grimstone at some point, and maybe even throt. But those seeds are much harder to find, and the plants are so fickle, I'm not certain I could coax them to blossom."

"Is that what all this is about? Jam?"

"Of course." He looked at her inquiringly. "Don't you like jam?"

"I love jam." The more she thought about it, the more fabulous it seemed, and the wilder. "So that's your business. The one you left Boston for, the one you've changed the zoning for."

"Yes." He pushed his glasses up and cleared his throat. "As long as I was throwing myself into this, I figured I might as well go all the way. It seemed as good a business as any." His mouth turned up into an apologetic lopsided smile. "It's strange, isn't it."

"Yes!" Gwyneth laughed, delighted beyond reason. "These jars, this weird book, these mind-bending poems, these ugly plants that make berries with ridiculous names. It's completely and utterly bonkers. And I'm completely on board."

It was Liam's turn to laugh. "You are?"

"Absolutely. It's the most wonderful, life-affirming thing I've seen since...well, since Tansy was born."

"I'm so happy you feel that way. It's quite a relief, you know. To have someone to talk to. It's hard to find someone to talk to, someone who won't judge. I have to admit I'm still a little shell-shocked. Not just from Maura. Just from life."

"Oh, believe me, I know that feeling well."

Liam's face softened. "Thank you for letting me share this with you. Gwyneth," he added, seeming to savor the word as it fell slowly off his tongue. His eyes locked with hers, and a subtle smile touched his lips. Gwyneth felt the smile in her eyes, but was incapable of smiling; something had shifted between them, but she didn't know how, and she didn't know what.

Her heart fluttered, and her blood warmed; she could no longer meet his eyes. Instead, she drifted back toward the store and let her gaze drift up to the lights, which sparkled like so many fairies above them. "What you've done is truly beautiful," she said as he joined her. "I admire you for giving up a life that wasn't satisfying for you, and recreating yourself in a life you desire."

Liam sighed. "Well, I sure hope so. I really don't know anything about gardening. Or jam, for that matter. I study, but studying's no substitute for doing. I learn as I go. Sometimes I feel like I'm doing this on a wing and a prayer."

"I wouldn't mind helping you," said Gwyneth, surprised by the forwardness of her words even as she was saying them. "That is, if it wouldn't be an intrusion."

"An intrusion? No. Oh, no! It wouldn't be an intrusion at all." His smile lines crinkled; his entire face brightened. "I'd appreciate the help."

"Okay." Gwyneth returned his smile, giddy as a schoolgirl. "I should probably go home, though. It's pretty late."

"Of course." Liam straightened, and his face turned serious. "Thank you for dinner. And for the company." He relaxed a little, and his voice softened. "It's nice to have a friend."

"It is." It really was. Warm contentment surrounded Gwyneth's heart. It was nice to have a friend; it was nice to have a secret. Gwyneth had always felt a little bit of a misfit; she'd blended into the background, subverting herself for her daughter, her parents, her fear of...of what? It wasn't rejection, exactly; it was more personal than that. Fear of happiness, which she didn't deserve? Of having needs? Of being noticed?

She smiled shyly and walked to the door; he followed and locked up after her. He walked with her to the steps of her porch. The night seemed darker, and the air colder; the snow had stopped, and reality had replaced the magic.

"Well," said Gwyneth. "Good night."

"Yes. Good night."

Slowly, she climbed the steps, her boots crunching the freshly fallen snow. She opened her door and looked backward. He smiled, waved, and ambled toward home.

CHAPTER SEVEN

The next day after work Gwyneth stepped out of her car and, rather than climbing the steps of her own porch, approached the door of Liam's barn. She hesitated a moment, then knocked three times, a merry little fluttering in her chest.

After a moment or two, the door swung open, and there he was, wearing charcoal slacks and a light gray sweater, a plaid gray collared shirt beneath. She straightened, inhaled, and smiled widely: she hadn't wanted to admit how much she'd been looking forward to seeing him. As usual, he had a comfortable, rumpled look, which wasn't unappealing—he looked like a man who in another life would be dapper, but in this one had too many important concerns to be bothered with matching or ironing. His tawny hair was pleasantly shaggy and mussed. Gwyneth imagined running her fingers through it—it was perfect hair for that, really.

"Ah! Hello, Gwyneth." He returned her smile and stood aside to welcome her inside. "I'm happy to see you. Please come in."

She stepped inside and looked about for changes since the night before. "Oh," she said, her eyes focused on a large ornate desk that clearly would serve as a register. "How beautiful this is." On the surface of the desk was a messy pile of sketches. She caught only a brief glimpse before he hurried to the desk and straightened the pile, then filed them away inside a drawer.

Gwyneth wanted to ask him about the sketches but didn't want to embarrass him, didn't want to reveal her own interest.

"How was work today?" he asked, reappearing from behind the desk.

"It was good." Gwyneth reached into her oversized woven bag and withdrew a long wool scarf, ivory in color, with a thick brown band. "I, um...I have something for you." She held her hand out. "Here."

His brow had risen, and he stared at the object in her hand. "This is for me?"

"Yes. I like to knit, and I knit a lot. The only problem is, I don't have a lot of people to knit for." She felt herself beginning to ramble; she made herself slow down. "Anyway, I have a lot of scarves and things, but none of them have a home." She smiled. "You're outside a lot, so I thought you could use it."

"Gwyneth, this is such a lovely gesture. Thank you." He looked at the scarf for a long moment, then wrapped it with reverential solemnity around the back of his neck, tossing one end over his shoulder.

"It looks nice on you," she told him, with an unexpected rush of glee. Indeed, it did: its understated, earthy colors were the perfect complement to his more vintage look, his old-soul eyes.

"Thank you." His eyes were warm and bright. They looked at each other for a moment or two. Gwyneth flushed and rubbed her lips together, feeling giddy.

"What are you working on?" she asked him.

"Oh." He started a little, glancing back toward his desk. "Oh, nothing of any importance. I was just...Well, it's rather silly, quite frankly."

"I'll bet it isn't." She smiled shyly.

He seemed to consider a moment, then returned her smile.

He chuckled. "Well, if you must know, I was attempting to sketch my labels."

"Labels?"

"For my jars. For my jam jars. A different illustration for each jam."

"Oh." Gwyneth's eyes lit up. "May I see?"

"Oh, I'm really not very good at all. They're nothing to get excited about, I assure you."

"Please," said Gwyneth, touching his arm once, with a playful little thrill. "Please let me see them. I'll bet you're better than you think you are."

Liam appeared to stifle a grin. "Okay," he said. "If you insist."

Gwyneth with effort contained her delight as he stepped back toward the desk to retrieve his papers from the drawer. He took them in his hand and placed them on the table, then stood back and waited for her to look through them.

Gwyneth took one in her hand. She stared at it, her eyes intent as they attempted to take it all in.

"Wow," she breathed.

"Do you like it?" she heard him ask her, though she didn't answer right away; she was entranced by the dragon in graceful flight, its scales painstakingly detailed, its wings spread about with wide majestic grandeur.

"Her eyes," whispered Gwyneth.

Indeed, Gwyneth was mesmerized by the eyes, which were unmistakably female: they were alert and beautiful, with a wisdom older than time.

She glanced at the pile on the desk and gasped, extending her hand.

"A fairy!"

She lifted the illustration and turned it toward the light, which cast the fairy in a golden, shimmery glow. Her limbs were long and delicate; her hair was wild and free. She sat on a flower, chin lifted, a small but potent power.

"What's this?" Gwyneth asked, picking up a paper with a small detailed design.

He peeked over the paper to see. "Oh, that's my logo."

"Mr. Mullany's rosette." Gwyneth smiled as she studied the design, recognizing the graceful shapes twirling and intertwining inside a quatrefoil. "I see you've added your personal touch."

"I made the lines stricter. And I exchanged the hearts for leaves."

"It's beautiful, so intricate. It reminds me of a mandala."

"That's exactly the look I was going for."

Gwyneth sifted through the rest of the illustrations. There were serpents, mermaids, forest animals dancing. Each was characterized by careful, lovingly placed lines, imparting to their subjects an intimate, sympathetic feel.

She replaced the last sketch on the table and stared at the pile, stunned.

"Wow," she said again.

"I do hope you like them."

"I love them." Gwyneth looked at him, her head cocked curiously. "Why do you think these are silly?"

"Dragons, fairies, bears dressed like people..." Liam laughed, playful humor in his eyes. "It's really something I do because it's calming. I don't know that I actually intend to use these."

"But why not?" Gwyneth's fingers brushed the pile on the table, reverentially tracing an eagle's wingspan. "They're so beautiful. You shouldn't be ashamed of them."

"Maura found them childish." He watched as she neatened the pile. "I don't generally share them."

"Well, I thank you sincerely for sharing them with me."

"And I thank you sincerely. For allowing me to trust you."

A weighty silence followed. She yearned to respond, but she couldn't even meet his eyes.

"Anyway, thank you for your thoughts," he said finally. "I really am glad you approve. I don't have a lot of time. I'd like to open the store on the twenty-fourth, and that's less than one month away."

"Oh, so exciting. So soon. Why the twenty-fourth?"

"There's a poem," he said. "In Llewellyn. About the number twelve." He reached toward the opposite wall and retrieved the book from a table, then stepped back toward her, his head bowed as he searched. "Aha." When he found it, he pointed, then handed her the book to see.

Twelve goddesses, joined by the hand,
Did dance upon the windswept sand.

Twelve voices from twelve tongues did rise,
Unfurling toward the starlit skies.

Twelve pairs of eyes closed to the night,
In witness of their inner light.

Twelve doth give peace, twelve doth give love;
Twelve, and all daughters thereof.

"I take 'all daughters thereof' to mean multiples of twelve," he said as Gwyneth passed the open book back to him. "I could be wrong, of course. Honestly, I just think it's fun to try to figure it out." He chuckled, then blushed. "I don't really know what I'm doing."

"I think it's lovely," said Gwyneth, looking up at him with an admiring smile. "And I agree. Multiples of twelve, definitely. And December twenty-fourth has them both."

"Yes, it does. So, I figured, why not open the store on that day. I can perform this little celebration ritual on the next page." He pointed, and Gwyneth tilted her head toward him to read. As she read, her face softened.

"It's so beautiful," she said, her eyes twinkling and her heart warming at the rich lyrics, written in appreciation of such special flowers.

"Don't worry; it's a fully clothed ceremony." He laughed, color once again creeping up his face. "If...If you wanted," he said quietly, pushing up his glasses, "you could join me." He pushed up his glasses again and cleared his throat. "If you wanted."

Gwyneth's smile shone in her eyes. "I'd love to."

He visibly relaxed, and his smile loosened. "Great." He hesitated a moment, watching her carefully. "Would you..." he ventured, "would you like to see the jam?"

Gwyneth lifted her face and smiled. "Yes, I would."

She followed him into the kitchen, where a jam-making process was clearly underway. Pots rested on burners, and rows of sanitized jars sat waiting to be filled with a rainbow of jams.

"Oh!" cried Gwyneth. "My, it smells delicious."

"Would you like to taste them? You can be my first."

Gwyneth nodded and smiled, her heart leaping as he offered her spoonful after spoonful of vibrantly hued jams. They were sweet, tart, earthy, and rich—each obscure flavor like a color she'd never seen.

Her favorite was a wine-colored jam with indigo seeds and a deep, spicy flavor.

"It's like royalty," she told him, her eyes fluttering closed.

"Like rubies and gold," he agreed, with a grin.

There were red jams, and orange jams, and yellow jams, and even blue. The prettiest jam was the pink one, like a ballerina's shoes.

"I think this one's the fairy. It's soft, like a fairy's touch."

"I think you're right. Maybe that's what I should name it."

At the end of the evening, Gwyneth reluctantly returned home; she didn't want to leave, but she worried about overstaying her welcome. Besides, Tansy was coming over. For reasons Gwyneth could not explain, she didn't want to tell Tansy about her strange friendship with Liam.

Throughout the week, upon returning from work, Gwyneth joined him in his garden to harvest the miraculous winter berries or helped him make jam in his kitchen. Sometimes he showed her new sketches; sometimes he asked her to test a new jam. Gwyneth was thoroughly enjoying herself: it gave her something to look forward to each day. She loved feeling a conspirator, performing secret rituals involving unknown flowers and sacred poetry.

One evening, Gwyneth found him in his barn as he was gathering his keys to leave. Her stomach lurched with disappointment.

"You're wearing your coat," she said. She swallowed and made herself smile. "Where are you going?"

"Oh. Yes," he said, looking down at his coat. "I was just on my way to collect my merrywort. It's supposed to be done during November's full moon. I'd invite you along, but..."

Gwyneth waited, a hopeful flutter of expectation in her chest.

"But what?" she asked tentatively when he didn't say anything more.

"Well, it's just that I'm supposed to... You may not... Well, there's part of the harvesting you may not like."

Gwyneth raised her eyebrows. "Why not? Is it painful?"

"Oh, no, nothing like that. It isn't painful at all."

Neither said anything. Gwyneth's hope began to falter.

"Would you..." he said then, his brow lifting, "would you *like* to come along?"

"Well," she replied, trying to disguise her eagerness, "only if you want me to."

"Oh, yes. Yes, of course." His brow now furrowed as he seemed to consider. "I suppose you could always wait in the car for...some of it."

"Okay." Now giddy, Gwyneth couldn't hold back a wide smile. An adventure? Great. A bonding experience with a new friend? Absolutely. "I'll go with you."

"Do you mind if I ask how long you were married?"

"I don't mind. I was married for six years."

"How long have you been divorced now?"

"About a year and a half. But the marriage was over long before that."

They were in Liam's old sedan, driving to Pierce's Cove, a little beach off the beaten track about twenty miles away. Bundled up in their warmest winter gear, clumps of snow melting around their boots and the rush of heat seeping from the vents, they embarked on their little journey beneath the indigo evening sky.

The intimacy of being so near him, in such close confines, enveloped by such warmth and enclosed by such darkness, and all so unexpectedly, made Gwyneth feel bold and alive. If they were going to be friends, she thought, should they not share a little more about themselves?

Gwyneth was curious, but she sensed she should tread carefully, wanting neither to upset him nor reveal the depth of her curiosity.

"How did you meet her?" she asked.

Liam pushed up his glasses and stared forward at the road, his thoughtful face bathed in shadows cast by the moonlight. "We met at a work event. Her firm was a client of my firm's. It was at a Christmas party." He paused a few moments. In that time, Gwyneth imagined him younger, neater, in a whole different life: dressed in a suit, hair not disheveled, the lines in his face perhaps more smile and less experience. "We were at the Houghton Plaza hotel. Super ritzy and all. I was speaking with a colleague by the punch table when I looked over toward the twenty-foot tree only to see a golden, glowing woman in an angelic ivory gown." For a second Gwyneth thought she saw a subtle smile touch his lips, but it was gone just as quickly. "At the time, I thought she was the most beautiful woman I'd ever seen."

Inside Gwyneth's chest was a low, powerful ache. Confounded somewhat by the intensity of her reaction, she sat in silence until it parsed itself out, or passed through her.

Liam seemed to grow extra still as he held the wheel. "At the time," he said again, pushing up his glasses.

Gwyneth looked at him. His face in profile was sober and serious. He was a thin man, and there was an angularity to his face that could have been stern. But there was softness in his features and sincerity in his eyes: his sparseness lent to them a certain candidness, and Gwyneth saw in him nothing but kindness.

"What happened?" she asked quietly.

"Well," he said, his hands tightly on the wheel, "I asked her to dance. Despite my social anxiety. I thought my comfort in doing so was some sort of sign that it was meant to be. And it was, at first. We danced the night away by the light of that tree. I made her laugh. She said I had character. She said she had never met anyone like me."

He pushed up his glasses, and Gwyneth thought about what he had said. She thought about her own life, how things that had seemed meant to be had turned out to be anything but—the naive, idealistic dreams of a young person who hasn't yet seen the world.

"For a while, we were very happy. At least, I thought we were. She was so elegant, well read...it felt surreal. But soon she began to grow frustrated. Maura is from a fine, influential family. I'm no good at parties. I say strange things. I embarrassed her. She started criticizing some of the things I did. The way I lined up the spices, the way I'm always pushing up my glasses." He laughed somberly. "I tried to stop it, but it was a losing battle. I have to pick my battles."

"I understand."

"My family kind of didn't. They pushed for me to work it out with her. They just didn't see that I couldn't. Not without changing who I was, at least. Or without completely losing my mind."

"Family can be tough like that."

They drove on in silence for a moment or two, the headlights parting the night like a velvet curtain.

"The marriage was stressful. There was this constant pressure, you see. To be something I wasn't, to hide my interests and to put on airs. She just couldn't understand my drawings. She thought they were too dark. They weren't anything terrible, really. I've always been fascinated with mythology. Like I said, she found them childish."

"They're neither terrible nor childish."

"I didn't think so." He pushed up his glasses. "Thank you."

A kind smile touched her lips. "So what happened?"

He shrugged. "She said she didn't want to be around me. I loved my wife. Too much, perhaps. And her criticism hurt me. I began questioning everything I was. I tried to change for her, to be there for her if I couldn't be what she wanted. I tried really hard. But then she said I was stifling her, that she needed her space. So I let her go. What else could I do?"

What else could he do, indeed. Gwyneth wanted to cry out that she knew, she knew. Her heart ached with secrets, secrets that burned a hole in her, leaving messy scars behind.

She could only offer what little solace she had. "I'm sorry," she said.

"I was, too. At the time." He paused momentarily and pointed to the side of the road. "Here we are. Pierce's Cove."

The car slowly glided onto the grass. To the right was a path leading into the trees. They swung the doors open and instantly were hit by a frigid, biting wind that rode the waves of the cold Maine sea. Gwyneth pulled her coat tighter around her body, tucking her chin into her collar and tromping with him into the dark forest.

They emerged on the other side of the trees onto the beach.

The full moon had cast an ethereal glow over the sand, which danced with the shadows of trees as they swayed in the winter wind. Ahead, Gwyneth saw the rocky Maine coastline; beyond, an inlet rippled and slapped against the shore until it emptied into the great sea and stretched to the black horizon.

Despite all her years of living here, Gwyneth had never been to the ocean at night, and certainly not in winter. She forgot about the cold and stared outward toward the sea, mesmerized by its dark, unknowable power.

Liam had taken a couple of steps toward the far side of the beach, but on finding she hadn't moved, he retraced his steps until he was beside her.

"It almost..." he said, "it almost seems alive."

Gwyneth nodded in agreement. The sound of the waves was steady, comforting. The sea was moving like a great murky monster. It was ominous, but beautiful.

"I'm sorry..." he said then. "I'm sorry to have learned of your husband's passing." He paused. "Do you mind if I ask what his name was?"

"His name was Grant. And we weren't married." Her voice was low, was nearly carried off by the wind toward the sea. In her belly was a wave of a different kind. She swallowed against the anxiousness she always suffered when she talked about this.

"Ah," he said then. "Right."

Gwyneth then offered the same words she'd grown used to offering, so many times it had almost grown easy. "He died saving a little girl from drowning."

Her eyes on the sea, she sensed him turning to look at her. When she herself turned to face him, she found him staring at her with wide, tender eyes.

"What a terrible tragedy. It must have been so painful."

"Yes." What was that she heard in her own voice? That darkness, that blended with the night?

"Does it help, at all, to know he died a hero?"

"I suppose it does."

The voice of the ocean was shrill in the harsh winter wind, yet she felt protected as they stood together within the moonlight's silver halo.

Gwyneth stared at the horizon, which seemed to sway with the waves. The ache in her chest was sharper now. Images from her past, long gone, jumped to the forefront of her consciousness. She wanted to say more; she knew, though, that she wouldn't, and she hated herself for her cowardice.

"Do you miss her?" she asked instead.

He didn't respond for a moment or two. Gwyneth stole a glance at him to find him watching the same horizon with a furrowed brow.

"I didn't want to get divorced," he said finally. "When she left me, I was so devastated I could barely get out of bed. I had thoughts...very dark thoughts. I started to wonder if the world really needed me here." He paused. "But in the darkness, there was relief. I think deep down I always realized that someone I was meant to be with would accept who I was, and love me for it. But I would never live up to what she wanted. Now I didn't have to."

He was standing with his hands in his pockets, his hair mussed by the wind. There was a quiet, unassuming strength in his stance, a wary confidence in the gentleness of his voice. The lines in his face revealed a history of laughing and suffering, of listening and knowing. Did he always have this power? Had she noticed he was this handsome? Gwyneth continued studying him, warming from the inside out.

He looked at her and smiled.

"To answer your question, then," he said, and offered her his hand, "I don't miss her. No."

Gwyneth reached out and let him take her gloved hand in his. Together, they trudged toward a line of trees in a shadowy grove, skirting the border of snow and sand. Gwyneth felt like she was in a dream, with the pressure of his fingers leading her, supporting her, in a way she hadn't known for so very long. To be supported, to be held—oh, but she missed being held! Had she ever truly been held? Or had she merely been held back? Gwyneth noticed their shadows on the moonlight-strewn beach. They stood side-by-side, connected in the middle, two conspirators in the night, the sound of their footsteps hushed by the snow and hidden by the sea. Gwyneth didn't know that she'd ever felt anyone's equal; she'd always had not enough power, or too much.

When he stopped beside a boulder, just before the entrance to the forest, she stood motionless, enchanted by the magic being created before her eyes. He withdrew his hand and bent toward the ground, digging in the sand until his hand emerged holding something that looked remarkably like a potato.

"What is it?" she asked him as he straightened and handed it to her. She took it in her palm and turned it over a few times, examining it.

"It's a merrywort bulb," he said, sounding a little in awe himself. "When I bought it, it was just a seed. The book said to plant it by a shady rock in the ocean air and that it would turn into a bulb. Now I go home and plant the bulb in my garden, and it'll grow berries that look like orange hearts." He stared at it. "I can't believe it actually worked, and so quickly."

Gwyneth was mesmerized. "Where did you get the seed from? Where do you get any of this stuff from?"

"It was the strangest thing," he said, his gaze on the bulb. "When I was looking to move, I was driving through the countryside, deep in the woods. I was just exploring. Out of nowhere, there was a cottage with a sign that said, 'Rare plants for a beautiful garden.'" He smiled as he remembered. "There was an old woman who lived there. I told her what I was interested in. She had it all." He took the bulb as she handed it back from him. "When I went back to visit her again, I couldn't find her. I was sure it was the right place." He shrugged. "But memory can be funny. I must have forgotten the exact spot."

"How mysterious and wonderful." She breathed in the crisp winter air, heavy with the musky scent of the sea. "Are you going back, now, to plant it?"

Liam was silent. His lips straightened, and he pushed up his glasses. "Not just yet," he said tentatively. "You see, I'm supposed to dance around the rock twelve times while reciting Merrywort's poem."

"Oh." Gwyneth's spirits lifted further; she liked the idea of participating in this magic. "Can I help?" She hesitated. "Unless another person's presence will break the spell."

"No, no. That's fine; that won't break the spell." He pushed up his glasses again. "It's just that I'm supposed to dance around the rock twelve times reciting Merrywort's poem, while naked."

Gwyneth's eyes widened, and she averted her gaze.

"You can wait in the car. I'll walk you there, and you can sit where it's nice and warm. I won't be long, I promise."

He cleared his throat and began walking away.

"I'll do it," she blurted suddenly, not giving herself time to change her mind. Her heart was hammering so hard she almost felt she would be sick; she made herself focus on her surroundings, deliberately feeling the frigid air to avoid passing out.

He turned slowly to face her, his expression blank. "What?"

"I said I'll do it." Odd how her nervousness was already dissipating, as was her horror at the boldness of her offer. Was it the magic in the air? she wondered, looking around at the night, at their seclusion. She looked him in the eye and managed a subtle grin. "That is, if you don't mind the company."

"No." He stood completely still, his hands at his sides and his tall form straight. "No, I don't mind."

"I know this dance is sacred, so I promise not to distract you."

He blinked a few times, remaining frozen for a beat; then he pushed up his glasses and strolled casually back toward her. "Oh, sure. Great. Thank you."

Awkwardly, he began removing his coat, which he laid at the edge of the forest. Averting his gaze, he pulled off his sweater, and Gwyneth, her heart stuck in her throat, did the same. *What have I done?* she asked herself frantically as out of the corner of her eye she noticed his fingers at the button of his trousers. She turned away from him and unhooked her skirt, for the first time remembering the fierce, biting cold. The area surrounding the boulder was mercifully free of snow, but the wind from the ocean struck her like knives. As she removed her undergarments and laid them on her skirt she huddled into herself, closing her eyes, so blinded by the cold she could barely even register her embarrassment.

Liam was unfolding a piece of paper, his body hunched and shivering. With wonder, Gwyneth observed him: he was subtly powerful, the tenseness of his stance accentuating his muscle's tendons and curves. With his skin bathed in moonlight, he looked mystical, otherworldly; Gwyneth was reminded of a classical statue, of the tenuous line between humanity and art.

He stood straight and bowed to the moon, which stoically seemed to accept his prayer. Then he began circling the boulder in long, graceful motions, his hands raised to the cloudy heavens. Through the shrieking of the wind Gwyneth recognized his gentle voice, meager against the crashing of the ocean, but strong enough to be heard, nonetheless. Gwyneth watched a moment, this naked creature worshipping in the night; then she bounded into the circle, arms about her, her graying red hair whipping in wild strands about her face. From behind her, she heard him chanting, and she chanted her own prayer, too; around her the sea wind seemed to lift her into the starlit sky, guiding her to do the goddess's bidding. Gwyneth no longer noticed the cold; she was one with the wind, the stars, the goddess, the night. She closed her eyes as she revolved around the rock, spinning like a planet around the sun that sustains her. Her prayer in time with his, their voices mingling and rising like smoke, Gwyneth felt in possession of all the secrets of the universe, like a free bird soaring above the mountaintops. When he slowed and stopped, their twelfth rotation complete, Gwyneth stood in a stupor, for a moment not understanding why the magic had suddenly vanished.

Gwyneth blinked and looked at him. He was breathing rather heavily. He was evidently unashamed, as unashamed as she; his arms were at his sides, and his body was straight and tall. They stood facing each other for what felt like a long time. Gwyneth was strangely at ease. She felt they were mirror images of each other—pure, naked counterparts beneath the black winter sky. She experienced a rush of emotion that was too complex for her to understand, or even to recognize.

Returning to the moment, he pushed his glasses up and shivered. "Okay then," he said. "We should get dressed before we freeze."

Slowly Gwyneth began to feel the cold again, and she dressed gratefully, wondering how she had born the wind so casually mere moments before. As they donned their coats, they glanced at each other, tossing each other shy smiles and excusing themselves as they clumsily bumped arms. Gwyneth was buttoning her coat, about to thank him for this otherworldly experience when he tapped her on the shoulder.

"There's one more thing," he said softly. "Will you join me at the water's edge?"

Gwyneth nodded and walked beside him toward the sea. They stopped just where the ocean met the shore. The last remnants of waves nipped at their boots.

"Now we thank the winter," he said, "for blessing us with a time for introspection and peace."

They stood for a minute or two. Gwyneth silently thanked the winter, which offered her an excuse for isolation, solemnity, and tea. Had she ever needed an excuse for any of those things? She pondered the winter that her life had become, cold, suppressed, and barren. Winter led to springtime, she considered. When would there be springtime for her?

"Do you need more time?" he asked her.

"No, I'm done."

She looked at the moon and its shimmery reflection in the ocean, feeling blessedly light and free. Holding her breath, she inched her hand toward his, and took it. He squeezed hers in return, and her lips parted, sending her breath into the air in a ghostly mist.

She braved a glance at him and was startled to find he was already looking at her. When their eyes met, he opened his mouth to say something, but never said it. The air between them seemed charged with electricity; Gwyneth didn't know whether to move closer or step away.

A gust of wind blew sand around them. They released each other's hands and covered their faces.

Gwyneth turned to him again, hoping to recapture the energy, but he was now looking at the horizon, his eyes wide and thoughtful.

She took a deep breath and turned back toward the sea. "What did you thank winter for?" she asked.

He pushed his glasses up. "I thanked winter for my garden, for my jam, and for giving me a new life." He turned to her. "How about you, Gwyneth? What did you thank winter for?"

Gwyneth had to wait to respond, for unshed tears were making her voice shaky. "I thanked winter," she said, "for sending me a friend."

"I WANT to thank you for joining me tonight," said Liam as he pulled off the shoulder and onto the road. The darkness of the night was complete, mitigated only by the headlights, which cut into the black but didn't dispel it. "It means a lot to me to be able to share this with another person." He paused a moment. "I hadn't realized how much difference it would make."

"I really enjoyed myself," she told him wholeheartedly, looking at him with a smile. "It was the most freeing experience of my life. I appreciate your trusting me with this very important responsibility."

"I don't know that I'd call it a responsibility, really. It's at best a boost to my wellbeing."

"That's a very worthy responsibility."

They drove along in silence. Gwyneth cherished the darkness, which seemed to bind them together, two spirits enveloped in the night.

"I'm thankful for the same thing you are, you know." He pushed his glasses up. "I just wanted to tell you that."

Gwyneth stared forward. It wasn't like the feeling she had when she spied on the workers from her window; it wasn't like the feeling of flirting shyly with men at the Historical Society. It wasn't even like the feeling when she'd received attention from Tansy's father. It didn't just bring a tingle to her skin, though it did that too: it was a feeling deep inside her, one of promise and hope.

They were approaching their street; soon their houses would appear. Gwyneth's hope was replaced with panic as the magical night's end grew near.

"Perhaps, when we get home," she hazarded, "you'd like to come over for some wine."

A moment or two passed before he replied. "Why, sure," he said, though his voice was unusually quiet. "I'd like that very much."

Gwyneth's heart was pounding, and her blood coursed furiously through her veins. The tension in the car was now palpable; somehow, she knew he'd understood. They said nothing as they turned onto their street, and as they drove through the snowy forest toward home her senses seemed to tingle and trill. She cast a glance in his direction: he was staring straight ahead, his expression very serious, his angular fingers clutching the steering wheel. In her mind's eye, Gwyneth saw him in his barest, purest form. She breathed steadily, her excitement nearly out of control.

At the sight of their houses Gwyneth exhaled smoothly, restless with anticipation, until she noticed the extra car in her driveway. Her eyes drew wide.

"Oh, no."

"What is it?"

Gwyneth didn't answer. A moment later, Liam noticed; he stared at the car for a beat or two, then pulled into his driveway without another word. They sat there in silence while they collected themselves.

"I suppose that's your daughter?"

Gwyneth closed her eyes, desperately forcing down a rush of dark, inexplicable anger. "Yes."

After a brief pause, he turned to her and smiled, though the smile fell short of his eyes. "Well, that's okay. We can...we can have wine another time."

She opened her eyes and looked toward the car, where Tansy sat waiting in the driver's seat. She looked at Liam and frowned.

"I..." she began. "I very much wanted you to come over tonight."

He blinked, his eyes remaining closed slightly longer than necessary. He appeared to take a deep breath. "I...very much wanted to."

Gwyneth could hardly hear him over the desperate pulsing of her heart. Under the spell of some unknown force, they leaned in toward each other. The slamming of a car door made them pull apart with a start.

"I have to...I have to go."

He nodded a few times, seemingly in a daze. "Okay," he whispered, and swallowed.

Gwyneth lingered a sad moment. Then, with a silent curse,

she threw open her door and met Tansy by her car. Tansy was holding a box of cookies from Gwyneth's favorite bakery. Gwyneth's irritation softened. On hearing Liam's car door shut, she turned to him, holding out her hand to introduce him to Tansy.

"Sugar, I don't think you've met Liam yet. Liam, this is my daughter Tansy."

"Hi," said Tansy, with a quick wave.

"Hello, Tansy," said Liam, coming to a halt beside Gwyneth and standing with his hands in his pockets. "It's very nice to meet you."

"Likewise. What have you two kids been up to?"

"Liam and I went for a little drive," Gwyneth answered, turning to Liam with a polite smile.

"Yes, that's right. A little drive."

"I was waiting for you," said Tansy, "but you were gone a long time."

"It wasn't that long." Gwyneth shrugged. "It wasn't that long, sugar, really."

"I need to talk to you, if that's all right. Here, I brought you a present for your troubles."

Gwyneth looked fondly at her daughter and took the cookies from her outstretched hand. "It was very sweet of you to do that."

"Hey, is that your new scarf?" Tansy fingered the scarf Gwyneth had finished knitting the previous evening. She looked at her mother, her expression pleasant and cheerful. "The one you learned that new stitch for?"

"It is. Do you like it?"

"It's gorgeous. Was the stitch very hard?"

As she spoke, Tansy made to head toward the house. Gwyneth hesitated, glancing backward at Liam, who was standing alone in the dark.

"Would you like to join us?"

"Oh," said Liam. "Thank you, but no. By that I mean, I

wouldn't dislike it, but you two should chat. Well." He pushed up his glasses and took a couple of steps back. "I'd better go." He waved at them and smiled. "Glad to meet you, Tansy. And..." His lips straightened, his face sobering. "Thanks for coming out with me. Gwyneth."

He waved once more and turned toward his house. Both women watched him go, Gwyneth aching with disappointment.

Tansy turned to her mother.

"He seems nice."

"Oh." Gwyneth indulged in a deep breath, preparing to put the magical evening behind her. "Yes. Yes, he's very nice."

"He's kind of cute, too," Tansy went on as the two made their way up the porch steps. "In an old, thrift store, nerdy kind of way."

"He's not old," Gwyneth protested, unlocking her front door. She pushed the door open and ushered her daughter inside. "He's only thirty-five."

"Thirty-five is old."

Gwyneth sighed and flicked on the light. She hung her coat on the coatrack and headed to the kitchen to put up some tea.

"He's no Daddy, of course." Tansy paused at the photo in the hallway. "And he's no Ken, either."

"Oh, is that who we're here to talk about?"

"Don't be silly, Ma. Ken is yesterday's news."

"Brian, then."

"Get with it! I'm with Alex now. I didn't tell you about that?"

"No." Gwyneth set two cups of tea at the kitchen table; Tansy brought the cookies. "What happened to Brian?"

"It turns out he had a girlfriend." Tansy nibbled on a cookie. "So that was the end of that."

"Oh." Gwyneth's eyebrows rose with surprise. She smiled at her daughter, her eyes crinkling with pride. "Good for you for not putting up with that."

"I wasn't the one who ended it," Tansy mumbled through her

cookie. She wiped her fingers on her napkin. "She found out about our date and put him on lockdown."

Gwyneth sighed loudly and slumped her shoulders. "Tansy..."

"I know, Ma." Tansy rolled her eyes. "You don't have to say it again."

"Well, apparently, I do."

"It wasn't my fault he lied to me."

Gwyneth studied her daughter carefully, her heart aching with both love and frustration. She was so utterly, wonderfully beautiful, and Gwyneth saw the golden soul inside. Despite her waywardness in relationships, Tansy tried to do her best. There was a childlike aspect to her approach to all things, one that prevented her from understanding the full meaning of her actions. Tansy would give you the shirt off her back, her heartfelt advice, your favorite cookies on a winter's night. But in matters of love, she saw no one beyond herself. Her life was a carousel of colorful men and temporary excitements, and she was oblivious to those around her who suffered in the path of her decisions.

She looks so much like her father, thought Gwyneth, not for the first time. Gwyneth often wondered how truly Tansy had suffered for not having a father. Did her resemblance to him reflect how much she needed him? Did he live on in her in a way that made her feel his absence more keenly? Gwyneth lamented that her daughter had never had a father; she believed his absence had left a void that her daughter had desperately attempted to fill. Tansy had begun dating young—too young, even younger than Gwyneth herself. At first her casual dalliances had seemed fluffy and fun, as puppy love should be. As Tansy matured, however, her love affairs had not, and Gwyneth always fretted that Tansy would never find what she was looking for.

"Tansy, sugar," said Gwyneth, taking her daughter's hand. "I wish you'd find a strong, stable man, one who doesn't need to cheat and who doesn't need to lie."

"I don't think that kind of man exists. Except for Daddy, but he was the exception."

"I just so desperately want you to be happy."

"Then lighten up, pass me another cookie, and tell me about your new scarf."

MIDNIGHT FOUND Gwyneth floating in her bathtub, her hands lightly treading the water, setting soft, silent waves lapping against her toes. She levitated her hips, making her body weightless as if she were a mermaid in the sea. There was freedom in weightlessness, a sense of existing, but claiming no space. The open curtains bore the sky, and Gwyneth could see Liam's bedroom window directly across from her own. The full moon her only witness, fresh snowflakes drifting through the cold night sky, Gwyneth smiled as she relished a newfound freedom, in her mind's eye seeing two worshippers dancing naked under that same watchful moon.

CHAPTER EIGHT

*G*wyneth awoke the next morning not knowing where dreams ended and reality began. Last night seemed like a fairy tale, a ballet she'd let sweep her away. She lay in bed for some time, relishing the memory, visions of dancers in her unopened eyes.

The light of day sobered her, and her bold suggestion seemed a product of magic that had been dispelled with the sunrise. She felt she should have been anxious about having made the friendship awkward. However, she was no longer sure he'd sensed her layered meaning; he'd never explicitly said so. Satisfied that she'd been sufficiently discreet, she resigned herself to going about her day as if it simply hadn't happened.

The sky was gray and overcast, and the silence in the air hinted of snow. Liam delighted her by showing up at the Historical Society right around lunchtime when she was answering emails at her desk. In his hand he held a picnic basket. He wore her scarf around his neck.

"What's this?" she asked brightly, affecting a more casual attitude than she felt. She stole a sly glance at him as he rested the basket on the table. She thought he looked especially happy today, his smile lines just a little more pronounced.

"Well, it was probably presumptuous," he told her, watching as she peered at the basket, leaning this way and that. "But I jammified that hollywot we harvested, and I thought I'd make us a lunch of it."

"How delightful!"

"Here I have some noddytom crackers," he said as he laid some rustic-looking flatbreads on a plate. "And here I have some goat cheese." He looked at her. "Obviously I didn't make this. I bought it at a cheese shop over in Asterfield."

"Of course. What else is in the basket?"

"Well, I might have been a little indulgent. When I was in Asterfield, I saw a chocolate shop. I brought us some almond-cherry bark. I hope you like it."

Gwyneth clasped her hands together and looked over the table like a little girl in a toy store. "Of course, of course. So where is the hollywot? What does it look like?"

"It's the strangest, wildest color." He pulled a jar from the basket and held it for her to see. "What do you make of it? Is that what you were expecting?"

"Good God, no." Gwyneth observed the coral-colored substance in the jar. It was shimmery, almost iridescent, seeming to sparkle beneath the glass. "You know what it looks like," she began. "It looks like a maple—"

"—like a maple leaf turning red in the fall."

A slow smile spread across her lips. "Yes."

He was smiling fondly at her, a conspiratorial twinkle in his eye. "I thought the exact same thing."

They spread the jam on the crackers and enjoyed a cozy indoor picnic, each delighted by the sweet, subtle flavor of the hollywot.

"It's like an elegant young lady in a modest dress," said Gwyneth, licking the tip of her finger.

"That's genius."

The sound of Leona's office door opening made them both turn.

"Oh," said Gwyneth. "Hello, Leona."

"What's going on out here?" asked Leona, eyeing the desk with interest.

"Um," Gwyneth stammered. "We were just finishing. We were very careful, I promise."

"Oh, I know. I don't care about that. I mean why wasn't I invited?"

"Leona," said Liam, swallowing a bite and rising to shake her hand. "How fortunate. I've been wanting to meet you. My name is Liam Baxter."

"Ah, yes. Our long-anticipated renovator. How do you like the house?"

"I love it. I love the house. Especially the turret."

"It's not a Victorian house without a turret! What did you do with that space?"

"It's a library. The contractor built bookshelves into the walls for me."

"Heaven on Earth."

Gwyneth listened with delight. She imagined the round turret library reaching toward the sky, and her heart pitter-pattered.

"Leona," said Liam, "please join us for some jam. I made it with hollywot from my very own garden. Gwyneth helped me harvest it."

"Hollywot, eh? It isn't going to kill me, is it?"

"Of course not," said Gwyneth. "It's delicious. Here, try some."

Leona cautiously drove the jam-covered cracker into her mouth, then closed her mouth and chewed. Her eyebrows rose, and her lips turned upward. "This is delicious," she mumbled through her mouthful. "It tastes like peaches."

"It does, a little," said Liam. "Now that you mention it."

"There's something else, though. Cinnamon? Or cloves?"

"No, just hollywot," said Gwyneth. "These special plants Liam cultivates produce berries with such complex flavors."

"Whatever it is, I've got peaches in the middle of winter. Go ahead and pass me another."

The three shared jam, crackers, and gossip about the town. Leona patted Liam on the back and brought him in for a brisk, firm hug.

"Welcome to Dearham, Peaches. It looks like you'll fit right in."

"I hope so," said Liam, pushing up his glasses. "Thank you for the warm welcome."

"When do you think you're going to open your shop? And what are you going to name it?"

"December twenty-fourth," he said definitively, standing straighter, his voice firm. "That's officially the day. As for the name, I haven't decided that yet." He scratched his chin thoughtfully. "I had a few ideas, but nothing's seemed right yet."

"Well, Gwyneth can help you. She's good at that stuff. In the meantime," said Leona, beckoning to Gwyneth with her finger, "you need to come with me. I have a principal arriving in ten minutes, and you and I need to go over a few things. He wants to talk to someone about a research project for his students."

"Okay," said Gwyneth. "I'll be right there."

Leona waved and exited; Gwyneth and Liam faced each other.

"Well," she said. "I'd better go."

"Sure."

She studied his face, so gentle and kind, his earthy eyes intent and sincere. She'd been attempting to hide from herself how much she liked him; she wondered why it had mattered so much.

"Are you..." she made herself say, and swallowed. "Are you going to be working in your garden tonight? By any chance?"

The pause that followed was almost imperceptible. "Yes," he said.

Gwyneth had intended to ask if she could help, but suddenly was bashful, not wanting to appear too eager.

He pushed up his glasses. "You could help me again, if you wanted."

"Oh," said Gwyneth, as if the thought had not occurred to her. "I'd like to, actually."

"You should know, though," he said then, "that I'm supposed to summon the snow."

He said nothing more, but the unsaid words hung in the air.

"That's okay," said Gwyneth. "I'll summon the snow, too."

GWYNETH WATCHED her window for signs of him. Just before midnight she saw him walking around the perimeter of his garden, wearing a bathrobe. He was holding the book and laying a hurricane candle holder at each corner. She reached him just as he was lighting the last candle. He stood straight and looked at her.

"We're all set," he told her, gesturing toward the garden. "This is a blossoming prayer, to help the merrywort grow. We follow the walls of the garden three times, then divide it into quadrants like a cross." He opened the book. "It's all in this poem, on page forty-four. I memorized it. But I have this flashlight"—he bent to the ground where a flashlight lay in the grass—"so you can see."

"Great."

He looked about a moment more, then met her gaze with a smile. "Okay, then," he said. "Let's do it."

He slipped out of his bathrobe, and Gwyneth did the same. Gwyneth's heart pounded as he approached her. Silently, he handed her the flashlight and the book. Gwyneth shone the light to the page. It was brittle and weathered with age, its delicate black script faded and cracking.

As she had the night before, Gwyneth waited for him to

begin. Then she fell in line behind him, reciting the magical poem, imagining Merrywort climbing from her bed.

THE SNOW NEVER CAME. After their recitations, they stood silently waiting for it, until the bite in the air forced them to dress and retreat inside, where Liam made them some tea. Gwyneth had never been in his house before; she'd only seen the barn. She admired the workmanship of the carpenters she'd watched for so many weeks, the hardwood floors and the tall ceilings, the restored wood around the doorways and windows. His house was sparsely but tastefully furnished, some papers and books strewn here and there but generally tidy and clean. They took their tea up to the turret and sat on a love seat by the window. Gwyneth looked about her with awe. In the scant light of the desk lamp, the books in their recessed shelves were gray silhouettes, guardians of secrets waiting for their time to be brought back to life. Outside were the treetops, and far below, the frozen ground —but above them was endless sky, clusters of stars visible through massive curving windows. It was an impressive, ethereal vision, and Gwyneth took it in reverentially. No less lovely was the vision of him, relaxed and content in her company, his smile bright but subtle, like the moon that cast shadows on the floor.

They chatted for a while, about all manner of things—mostly Maine, family, and personal pains and joys. Though entranced by the intimacy of the evening, Gwyneth knew she had to leave; it was, by now, well after midnight, and she would be exhausted in the morning.

They expressed sincere gratitude for the company, each pausing too long as if waiting for the other to say more. As Gwyneth turned away from him and walked down the steps of his porch, she glanced backward at him once more. He was watching her go, his face very serious. Upon meeting her gaze, he smiled warmly, and he waved as she crossed the lawn toward home.

GWYNETH JOINED him every night that week. They dutifully followed the poem's rules, dancing among the blossoms or chanting as they faced each other by a flourishing Aedrian's Star. Gwyneth could feel something building, something certain, that was taking its time. She lived for the freedom of their dancing, for shedding her defenses and celebrating herself. And though they always seemed to end the night with a question, in the garden, they were pure as the goddesses they summoned.

He visited her at work one day, bearing five jars of sherryweed jam.

"I conducted some experiments," he told her, at her invitation unloading the jars on her desk. "Various levels of sweetness, some with honey, some with fruit. I was hoping you'd help me decide which is best."

"I can help you, Peaches," called Leona, who quickly appeared at her door. "Is there enough there for three?"

"There sure is, Leona." Liam waved her over. "I could use your opinion, too."

The three of them talked jovially over crumpets and jam, rating each variation on its flavor, texture, and smell. They settled on sherryweed and honey, then relaxed until lunchtime was over.

Leona returned to her office. Liam and Gwyneth packed up his basket; then they rose so Liam could take his leave.

"I'm sorry to say I won't be gardening tonight," said Liam. "Llewellyn is explicit that tonight is for rest. But maybe you could come over for tea again, anyway." He pushed up his glasses. "If you'd like to, of course."

Gwyneth smiled. "I'd truly love to, but my daughter is coming for dinner." Her brow rose hopefully. "You should join us."

"Oh," he said. "I don't want to intrude."

"You're not intruding. I want you there."

"Oh." He returned her smile, his eyes shining with irresistible boyish joy. "Okay, then." He pushed up his glasses; his voice seemed brighter than usual. "I'd love to join you for dinner. I'll be there."

～

"So I TOLD Alex I didn't think we should be exclusive," Tansy was saying as she and Gwyneth set the table for dinner. "The chemistry just wasn't right. There wasn't any spark, you know what I mean?"

"But Tansy," said Gwyneth, frowning, "Alex seemed so good for you. You said he was a really nice guy."

"Yeah, maybe that's it. Maybe he was too nice." Tansy placed the second plate down and looked at the third in her hand. "Here, Ma," she said, handing it to her mother. "You gave me an extra plate."

"No, I didn't," said Gwyneth, willfully suppressing the exasperation that was about to burst out of her throat. "Liam is coming for dinner."

"You two have gotten pretty chummy." Tansy raised her eyebrows. "Eh, Ma? How chummy are you two?"

"Oh, stop it," Gwyneth chastised, more forcefully than she'd intended. "He's just a friend. He's all alone here in Dearham, and I invited him for dinner."

"Gosh, no need to get so defensive. I was just wondering if you liked him."

"Of course I don't. Not like that, anyway. Why do people always assume a man and a woman can't be just friends?"

Tansy shrugged and walked back toward the kitchen. Gwyneth stood there for a moment, staring at the centerpiece, for the first time fully understanding that what she'd said was a lie.

The doorbell rang; Gwyneth turned to the mirror above the sideboard and frantically straightened her frizzy graying ponytail. As the front door creaked open she unbuttoned the collar of her sweater—why did she dress like an old widow?—and untied her scarf, instead letting it hang around her neck and one shoulder. On a whim, she pulled out her ponytail, letting her hair tumble down her sides. Suddenly, everything mattered. *How do I do this?* she asked herself, not receiving any answers. She took a deep breath and waited for him to appear.

Tansy entered first, chattering away, and then there he was, straight and tall, a large jar in his hands.

"Liam brought jam," said Tansy, reaching for the wine and pouring three glasses.

"Oh," said Gwyneth. "Thank you." She attempted an awkward smile. "You can put it on the table."

"I really hope you like it," he said, seemingly oblivious to her torment. "It's the merrywort," he added with a grin.

"Merrywort!" Gwyneth forgot her awkwardness and stared at him. "It grew that quickly!"

"Unbelievable, isn't it?"

"But it didn't even snow that night."

Liam shrugged his shoulders, a genial smile on his face. "As I said, I don't really believe in the poems." His smile gentled. "I think maybe, like poems, a garden's more about passion than rules."

Gwyneth tingled all over. "Should we sit down for dinner?" she asked, and turned away to hide the blush that had turned her crimson.

She brought her roast chicken to the table and served everyone. They all dug in, Tansy and Liam complimenting her on the meal.

"Gwyneth, your cooking soothes my soul," said Liam, eating heartily, and smiling.

Gwyneth flushed, warmth flooding her. "What a lovely thing to say, Liam. Thank you."

"My mom's an amazing cook," said Tansy, through a mouthful. "She tried to teach me, but I never got the hang of it."

Gwyneth chuckled. "That's why you come home for dinner so often, sugar."

"I must take after my father, because I've got no skills." Tansy sipped her wine. "What do you think, Ma? Could Daddy cook, or was he as bad as I am?"

"Worse."

Tansy laughed. "Oh well. I guess he couldn't be good at everything he did. He used up his gifts on his looks, right?" She turned to Liam. "My dad looked just like Van Donnelly."

"Ah."

They ate a moment in silence. Gwyneth and Liam's eyes met, and his smile grew serious. Gwyneth looked back down and smiled into her dinner, unable to hold his gaze.

"Hey, Ma," said Tansy. "How come you took your hair down? You hardly ever wear it down."

"Oh." Gwyneth patted her hair, flustered. "I don't know. I just felt like it."

"Well, it looks really pretty. Doesn't it, Liam?"

"Yes, it does," said Liam, pushing up his glasses. "I agree with Tansy."

"You see? Liam agrees with me."

"Liam is very agreeable."

Nobody said anything, the clinking of their forks against their plates the only sound.

"This really is good, Ma," said Tansy. "It's great comfort food. Perfect for after a long day at work."

"Was it a long day, sugar?"

"The longest." She turned to Liam. "I work at The Salty Seashell in Bar Harbor. Have you been there?"

"I haven't, not yet."

Tansy took a long sip of wine. "It's a cool place, but lately I've been feeling kind of stagnant. My boss is a nightmare. I may start looking around."

"Oh?" Gwyneth had perked up, and she regarded her daughter with interest. "What about nursing school?"

"Yeah, about that. I don't think I want to do it anymore. It's just not something that interests me all that much."

"I know it would be difficult, but—"

"It's not about it being difficult." Tansy's face had hardened slightly, but she quickly recovered, and smiled. "I just don't want to do it. You know?"

No one spoke; the air was tense. Thankfully Tansy diffused it, with her ebullient smile turning once again to Liam.

"Liam," she said, leaning back in her chair with her wine. "What's with that big ugly plant in the middle of your garden?"

"Oh." Liam once again pushed up his glasses, straightening. "Well," he said, "that's Aedrian's Star."

"Who's-it's what's-it?"

"Aedrian's Star," he repeated, smiling politely. "That's the name of the plant."

"I've never heard of it. Why is it there?"

"Tansy," interjected Gwyneth.

"Oh, I don't mind." Liam offered a gentle smile; Gwyneth smiled back, relaxing.

Liam turned to Tansy. "You see, it's mentioned in a book I'm reading. It interested me, so I decided to grow it myself."

"A book? What book?"

"A poetry book."

"I don't read poetry."

"It's really a lovely book," said Gwyneth, a little nervously, possessive of their secrets. "Liam showed it to me. We've read part of it together."

"Well, maybe I can read it, too." Tansy smiled. "I said I *don't* read poetry, not that I didn't *want* to read poetry."

The two women looked at Liam, who pushed up his glasses and shifted in his seat. "Sure," he said to Tansy. "I can show it to you, if you'd like. Maybe not until my store opens. I'm trying to preserve a little mystery."

"Your store? What store is that?"

"I'm opening a jam store in the new barn, and I'm using my own garden for ingredients."

"That's cool. Like a farm-to-table restaurant."

"I suppose so, yes. Perhaps you might call it a garden-to-jar shop."

Tansy laughed. "Garden-to-jar shop. That's funny. Well, if you showed the book to my mother, you can show me too. I can keep a secret. I promise."

A few silent moments passed as they awkwardly swallowed a few more bites.

Liam cleared his throat and turned to Tansy once more.

"Did you know, Tansy," he began, "that your mother is not only a wonderful cook, but also a gifted gardener?"

"I didn't know that," said Tansy, elbows on the table, dabbing her fork at him to emphasize the point. "How, may I ask, do you?"

"Oh, Gwyneth has been so helpful," said Liam, looking at Gwyneth fondly. "She's helped me plant and harvest the berries for my jam. She's also helped me in the kitchen. I think her touch has made the jam much sweeter."

"That's awesome," Tansy said, smiling with delight. "My mom is pretty sweet."

"It's the berries," whispered Gwyneth, embarrassed, but elated. She cleared her throat, forcing herself to sound normal. "The berries in the garden are just naturally very sweet."

"Well," said Liam quietly, averting his gaze as he speared a piece of chicken, "I greatly enjoy the company, in any case."

Gwyneth was growing more and more certain she wasn't imagining the meaning behind everything he was saying. She looked at him as he pretended to be casual; she could tell he was pretending by the way he was lining up his napkin along the edge of the table. Gwyneth sensed a change in the air, like the first halo of gold peeking over the eastern horizon. For the first time in years, it seemed, hope grew in her heart.

"Ma," said Tansy; Gwyneth looked at her blankly, still emerging from her thoughts. "I don't get it. Why didn't you tell me you were doing any of this? You didn't even tell me your neighbor had a shop."

"I don't know," said Gwyneth. Why hadn't she, anyway?

"It was sort of a secret," said Liam, mercifully intervening. "I asked her not to tell."

"Well, now I know," said Tansy. "How fun!"

The subject turned to other things, and Gwyneth relaxed, relieved. Tansy would think it was silly, that she herself was silly. But it was more than that. The truth was, she supposed—the truth was that she was selfish. She wanted this for herself. She didn't want to explain herself, answer anyone's questions, hear anyone's advice. She liked having a secret; it made her feel special, like something she did mattered. She wanted something with only him; she wanted him to depend on her and her alone.

After dinner, Tansy stayed behind while Gwyneth walked Liam up to his door. They stood facing each other on the front porch, their breath white tufts between them. Gwyneth had too much to say, and too little. She was grateful when he began, looking her square in the eye as he spoke.

"Gwyneth," he told her. "I have a confession."

He was watching her very seriously. Gwyneth dared barely to breathe.

"I've grown," he began, and swallowed, "very fond of you."

Though she'd been hoping for it, she didn't yet believe it; surely she heard more in his words than he'd intended. She stood in silence, heart racing, waiting for him to say more.

"I..." He paused a moment, appearing to gather strength. "I think about you. Quite often."

Gwyneth felt her eyes soften; her heart, meanwhile, seemed to flutter and fly. Gwyneth thought about him, too, more than she'd admit, more than she'd admitted to herself. She'd begun to feel a little dizzy, and she couldn't meet his eyes; her gaze rested on their feet, and at the sight of his shabby, lumpy brown shoes, she couldn't help but smile.

"I think about you, too," she told him, now meeting his gaze, starry-eyed. She'd thought of him in her bathtub, as she floated beneath the stars; she'd thought of him as she stared out her window, wondering when he'd appear. She'd thought of him as she sat at her desk at work, imagining him pushing up his glasses or offering her his earnest smile. She'd thought of his kindness, his deference to her feelings, how he'd been hurt for being himself and how she wanted to make him feel wanted. She'd thought of him constantly, his straight, linear form, the strength of him hidden beneath drab, old-fashioned clothes.

She felt herself drifting, her arms moving upward; then his face was in her hands, and she was standing on tiptoe parting his lips with her own. *So soft*, sighed Gwyneth, spurred by his eager response; the kiss, like he himself, was deceptively gentle, latent energy beneath. It was this understated strength that drew her...this vulnerability in a staunch soul. She kissed him more deeply, enticed by his scent and his taste; they were deep, and uniquely masculine, as vital as his movements were tender. As he moved with her in a slow, steady rhythm, his lips warm and ready and his hands now bunching, subtly, her coat around her waist, Gwyneth felt herself melting, allowing herself to be taken, allowing herself to take.

He pulled his lips from hers, but remained close, his forehead resting on hers. His breathing was deep but steady. He moved his hand to the side of her face, and Gwyneth's knees wobbled at this gentle gesture of need.

"Come inside with me," he whispered, his breath heavy on her lips.

Every nerve in her body screamed for her to say yes. Oh, how she desperately, urgently wanted to! And how good it was to be asked! How exquisite to share this intimacy with him, to be desired by him and to burn with desire, too.

"But Tansy," she uttered, struggling to remain standing.

He closed his lips and nodded, seeming to catch his breath. "Right. Of course." He made a valiant attempt to smile.

Gwyneth hesitated, then smiled coquettishly. She cradled his lower lip with her own, drawing from him a deep, if reticent, sigh. "Well," she said, "maybe I can come back when she's gone."

He kissed her gently, then rubbed her back with his hand. "Of course," he said again, quietly, though Gwyneth sensed his excitement. "Whenever you're ready, I'm here."

"Jeez, what took you so long?" asked Tansy, who was washing the dishes at the sink. "Did you get lost?"

"No." Gwyneth had composed herself before walking into the house; she hoped her giddiness wasn't evident on her face. "We were just saying good-bye."

"Well, I'm glad you finally did. Something's happened, and I'm just so excited to tell you."

"Oh?" Gwyneth placed her hand on her daughter's shoulder and kissed her cheek, then took up the dishes she was washing, to dry them. "What's that, sugar?"

"I've found a new man. And he's a good one, too. It's like it was meant to be."

"Really?" asked Gwyneth, absentmindedly, used to Tansy's animated recitations of her romantic escapades. "Who is it?"

"Liam."

Gwyneth froze, a porcelain serving dish in her hand. She turned slowly to face her daughter.

"What?"

"Ma, think about it. It's perfect. You keep saying I need to find myself a good man. Well, Liam's nice, right? Not like the others?"

"Ye-es." Gwyneth put the dish down and gripped the countertop.

"Ma? Are you okay?"

"Yes." Gwyneth fortified her face and resumed drying the dish, making her voice calm and casual. "You think you like Liam, do you?"

"Well, he's not my usual type, I'll admit," said Tansy brightly. "But I think you're right that I'm due for a change."

"I'm not sure Liam's looking for a relationship." Gwyneth clawed desperately at responses, saying the first things that came to mind. "He just moved here. He just got divorced. I think he wants to get settled before putting himself out there again."

"If he's divorced, that means he's not married." Tansy smiled, pointing her finger at her mother. "You keep telling me to stop dating married men."

"If you want, I'll talk to him. I can ask him how he feels."

"Oh, I already know how he feels. It's so obvious he's interested in me!"

Gwyneth stared at her, the pit in her gut growing heavier by the second. "It is?"

"Of course it is! Just think about it." Tansy took a pot in her hand and scrubbed the inside, her shiny sable hair cascading over her shoulder. "You heard the way he kept making a point of talking to me, asking me questions and telling you he didn't mind that I was questioning him about that poetry book."

"I think he was just making conversation."

"What, is it so hard to believe he'd be interested?"

"Of course not, sugar. That's not what I meant."

Tansy had stopped working a minute to turn to her with a

frown. She now resumed her washing, passing Gwyneth the pot and picking a glass from the counter. "You think he's too nice for me. I get it."

"Tansy, now, stop."

"I just don't see why you keep arguing with me. I want to pursue this. I think there's something there."

Gwyneth watched her daughter, so lovely, so full of life. *Is there?* wondered Gwyneth, her mind working furiously to recall the events of the night. He'd said he was "fond" of her, that he thought of her "quite often." Had she misinterpreted? Had she assumed he'd meant more than he did because she'd wanted him to? Maybe he knew she was lonely; maybe that's why he let her help him with his jam. Maybe what he felt for her was empathy, or even worse, pity. Sure, they had kissed, and a good kiss it was, too. But really, she'd kissed him first; what man in his shoes wouldn't act as he had?

"Ma?"

Gwyneth mechanically dried the glass, not even seeing it as she held it in her hands. *What would he want with me, anyway,* she wondered, *a silly old woman spying from her bathroom window?* She'd been foolish to think he could see her any differently; it was the dying dream of a spinster past her prime. She caught a reflection of herself in the window, took a lock of her hair in her fingers and studied it. *So much gray*, she thought with a sigh. *So much time passed, a string of indistinguishable days one after the other. And for what?*

"Ma. Ma! You're totally spacing out. Are you okay?"

Gwyneth turned and looked at Tansy. It didn't even matter if she'd been wrong or right; it didn't matter why he'd kissed her or if his thoughts of her were as tender as were her thoughts of him. Tansy was her daughter; her happiness came first. She couldn't risk confrontation with Tansy—not after years of secrecy and lies. And besides, eventually, she'd had to have told him the truth. She consoled herself that she'd saved herself that misery, saved him the trouble of rejecting her.

"I think that's wonderful, sugar," she whispered, voice breaking. "I'm sorry—I have a really bad headache. I'll see you tomorrow, okay?"

∾

GWYNETH PEERED out her bathroom window at the light in Liam's living room. A shadow moved, from time to time, on the other side of the curtain. He was waiting for her.

She'd emerged from her bathtub ten minutes ago; she'd been standing here in her robe all this time. Somehow, she couldn't go to sleep yet, knowing he still expected her.

Try as she might to convince herself he didn't really want her, that he'd only been drawn by her eagerness and had responded with nothing more than lust, it continued to sound like a lie. Part of her knew it was an excuse, and allowed it—the part that was frightened, that had never done this before. *Forty-seven years old*, she scolded herself, *and frightened like a schoolgirl*. But a schoolgirl was what she was; a schoolgirl was what she had been the last time she'd let her heart go. It had gotten her a daughter, her greatest treasure on Earth—and crippling anxiety that had prevented her from letting it go since.

Goddammit, she cried internally, as tears pricked at her eyes. She didn't deserve it anyway; she'd led a sheltered, selfish life. What did she do for anyone, besides Tansy? And hadn't she already hurt Tansy enough? Tansy, her only confidante, her daughter, her playmate, her friend. Wasn't it Gwyneth's fault Tansy had searched so long for stability—hadn't it been her choices that had made Tansy so vulnerable in the first place? Gwyneth wouldn't do it again; she wouldn't take more from her daughter. A mother's job was to protect her child, even more so when she'd bequeathed to her child the repercussions of her own mistakes. Gwyneth was resigned to loneliness; she'd given up years before. But Tansy was young, with her whole life in front of her. She was pretty and fun.

She was probably better for him anyway. If Tansy wanted to pursue him, what right did she have to stop her?

The shadow moved, and the light went out. Gwyneth wiped her eyes on her sleeve and shuffled off to bed.

CHAPTER NINE

*I*n the morning, Gwyneth sneaked out of her house carefully, terrified of running into Liam. She had no idea what she would say to him, how she would explain not returning last night. She couldn't tell him she was giving him up for Tansy. But it would kill her to lie about her feelings, and it would hurt his feelings, to boot. Never one for confrontation to begin with, Gwyneth felt herself nearly sick with fear. She peeked outside warily to make sure the coast was clear, then scrambled to her car and pulled hastily away.

So it was with an agitated lump in her gut that she heard the bell tinkling as she sat at her desk, only to look up from her paperwork and find him standing there watching her, his trusty basket in hand, her scarf hanging over his neck.

"Oh, Liam," she said, trying, and failing miserably, to act as if nothing had happened. "What a...it's so nice to see you."

He approached her slowly, with a kind little smile. "It's nice to see you, too," he said. He paused. "Are you busy? I don't want to—"

"No, I'm not busy," she interrupted, sounding somewhat

manic. She indulged in a deep breath and attempted a smile. "Do you want to have a seat?"

"I brought some sandwiches." He put the basket on her desk and opened it, then removed two paper bags. "There's one for you, one for me, and one for Leona in the basket. Peanut butter and throt. I was so excited, I couldn't resist coming down here to share it."

"Throt?" she asked brightly, momentarily forgetting her discomfort. "You harvested the throt!"

"Yes." His smile widened, and Gwyneth's heart squeezed; his boyish joy was contagious, and she couldn't help but share his pride. "It's a miracle it grew, and as abundantly as it did. Llewellyn said it would come quickly. It was overnight, quite literally overnight. I woke up to it this morning. I couldn't even wait, I had to try it right away."

"You must have a knack for it." Gwyneth's eyes twinkled; she gestured with her hand to sit. "Leona's on a conference call. I'll make sure she gets her sandwich." They each took a sandwich. Liam held his out to hers.

"To throt," he said, touching her sandwich with his own.

"To throt," she repeated, and took a wary bite.

Instantly their eyes met, and they broke into wide, happy grins.

"It's delicious!" she exclaimed, looking at the sandwich with wonder.

"It is, isn't it? I should try it with the angel herb."

"Mmm," she agreed, nodding, her mouth wrestling with the peanut butter. She swallowed and sipped her coffee. "You should write a recipe book. I'll bet it would do really well."

"That's not a bad idea, though the ingredients are so obscure. What fruit, do you think, can substitute for throt?"

"That's true. There's no replacement. Throt's in a class by itself."

They ate in silence for a minute or two. Gwyneth was in agony wondering what he was thinking. Was he angry, or indifferent, or hurt? Was he simply not going to mention it?

She was just beginning to think she wouldn't have to talk about it when he set down his sandwich and faced her.

"Gwyneth, I came here to apologize," he blurted.

She looked up at him with surprise. "You what? Why?"

"Because I put pressure on you." He pushed up his glasses and looked at her with a frown. "I shouldn't have suggested what I did. What a tough spot I put you in. I hate that I made you uncomfortable." He shook his head ruefully. "I'm so embarrassed. And so sorry."

"Oh, no," said Gwyneth, putting her sandwich down and shaking her head vehemently. "No, no, no. You have nothing to be sorry about."

"I absolutely do. I wanted to apologize when you didn't come back last night, but I was too ashamed to do it. What a coward I am."

"No." Gwyneth reached across the table and rested her hand on his; warmth sparkled through her veins and across her skin, and she removed it instantly. "Please don't beat yourself up. I don't want you to feel badly about it."

"Well, I do. You clearly weren't ready."

"It's not that I wasn't ready."

He said nothing, seeming to be working out the meaning of her statement. Perhaps he heard it in her voice; he seemed to sense that more was coming and that it would make things more complicated. His gaze intensified as he waited for her to go on.

Gwyneth took a deep breath and firmed herself. "I can't be with you," she said.

He blinked and stared at her with an inscrutable expression. "Okay."

She bit her lip, her fingers fretting nervously with her pencil.

"Do you mind..." he said then, pushing up his glasses and shifting in his seat. "Do you mind if I ask..."

"I don't mind if you ask, but I can't give you an answer."

He thought about this, his lips drawn downward. "Was it the kiss?"

"No."

He closed his eyes a moment. "I'm sorry. You certainly don't owe me an explanation."

Neither said anything for quite some time. Gwyneth looked around the empty office. Behind her, she heard the muffled sounds of Leona pacing her office as she talked on the phone.

"I..." he said finally. "I think you're really special. Gwyneth." His jaw worked. He attempted a sad smile that didn't reach his eyes, and a tender ache seized her heart. "I'm happy to have you as a friend." He cleared his throat and pushed up his glasses, then sat up straighter, attempting to recover. "If you'd still like to join me for the applethistle harvest, I'll be outside a few minutes before midnight tonight. And of course, you're still invited to the Ceremony of Twelve the midnight before opening night—"

His voice trailed off as he noticed Gwyneth shaking her head.

"I'm afraid I can't help you with your garden anymore, Liam."

His face fell, and Gwyneth closed her eyes against the sight of his disappointment. He didn't deserve this pain, and she'd never hated herself more. *Goddammit,* her heart cried, pounding with frustration, pain, and what she vaguely recognized as anger. She opened her eyes and met his gaze, ready to face her obligation. She didn't know for whom she was sadder, Liam or herself.

"Oh," said Liam, his kind, boyish face turned downward. He shifted again, in agitation; Gwyneth felt she could see the open wound of his marriage through the earnestness of his eyes.

"I don't want to hurt your feelings," she told him desperately, though she was completely aware of the emptiness of her words.

"It's fine, Gwyneth. It's really, truly fine." He smiled now, too brightly, and brushed his hands of crumbs. "You know, I forgot I have an appointment. Would you mind terribly if I eat and run?"

"No." Gwyneth stood as he stood, watching him gather his

things. He threw on his shabby brown coat, which hung loosely over his tall straight form. "Good luck with your garden, Liam."

"Thanks so much, Gwyneth. And thanks for all the help you've given me! You really were a huge help." His hand shot up in an abrupt, awkward wave. "Have a good day. You were a huge help."

With that, he turned and walked out, the door tinkling behind him.

Gwyneth sank into her chair, her head in her hands, her fingers raking through her hair. She sucked in her breath and held it, overcome with crippling nausea. She had thought deeply about whether to continue their friendship and had come to the conclusion that given the direction in which their relationship had been heading, it would be too hard for her to see him again at all. She'd been dreading having to tell him, had known it would be difficult, but knowing she was the cause of his suffering was a sharper, more profound pain than she'd ever thought possible.

"Goddammit!" she muttered, and wiped her eyes with the heels of her hands.

"God damn what? Was that Peaches who just left?"

Gwyneth quickly sat straighter, hiding her face in her hair. "Yes," she choked out.

Leona was staring at her, paper coffee cup in hand. "What's the matter?"

Gwyneth closed her eyes to hold back tears. "Nothing," she whispered, unconvincingly.

"Sure doesn't look like nothing to me." Leona said nothing for a moment; her head bowed, from behind her hair, Gwyneth could sense her standing there thinking. "Why did Peaches leave without saying hello? And did he leave any jam?"

"Here." Gwyneth sighed and pushed the sandwich toward the edge of her desk. "He brought this for you."

"He's always so thoughtful!"

Gwyneth said nothing. Having calmed somewhat, she

straightened, tucked her hair behind her ear, and made a pretense of poring over her paperwork.

"You sure you're okay?" asked Leona.

"I just had a little tickle in my throat," Gwyneth said, clutching her throat as evidence. "But thank you."

Leona retreated to her office to take a phone call. Gwyneth sat for a while with her elbow on the table, her chin in her hand, watching the snow beginning to fall outside the window. *Moriander must be pleased,* she thought, smiling for a moment at the memories of her midnight harvests. Fresh tears welled in her eyes, and she straightened, sighed, and forced herself to get back to work.

CHAPTER TEN

Gwyneth wandered through rows of Christmas trees, watching the sway of her skirt and pretending she wasn't at a local farm but back at Pierce's Cove, dancing on the edge of the forest. She inhaled slowly and deeply, taking their pungent fragrance into her lungs and relishing the brief solitude.

"Ma, where are you? What about this one?"

Gwyneth closed her eyes and tried to gather her wits. It had been difficult for her to be with Tansy, to watch her shamelessly flirting with a man she neither understood nor, Gwyneth suspected, truly cared about. For the last few days, since Liam had made his quick exit from the Historical Society, Gwyneth had held her tongue as Tansy blithely excused herself from her visits to help him in his shop, unloading boxes, setting up the register, arranging signs, and organizing displays. She also talked to him as he worked in his garden, though she didn't help him with that: Tansy had no interest in getting her clothes dirty.

"There you are." Tansy's bright, smiling face appeared around the corner. She was wearing a stylish brown coat, an ivory hat, red gloves, black jeans, and tall boots. Her perpetually glossy hair fanned out over her shoulders. In the distance, the mountains rolled in hazy purple waves. It was a picture-perfect moment, a beautiful girl among beautiful, festive scenery. "Where did you go? Are you hiding?"

"No," said Gwyneth, stepping toward her, dried pine needles crunching beneath her feet. "Of course not."

"Well, come over here. I think I found the perfect one."

Gwyneth sighed internally. It seemed Tansy was always saying she'd found the perfect one.

They stopped before a stout blue spruce. Tansy stood before it and ruffled its branches.

"So what do you think?"

"Hmm," said Gwyneth solemnly. "I prefer Scotch pines."

"I know you do, Ma. But you always get one, and you always complain about the needles. Maybe it's time to try something new."

Gwyneth stared at Tansy, with her sparkling eyes and her carefully made-up face. As she watched her, Tansy raised her brow inquiringly.

"Scotch pine," said Gwyneth, and began to walk away. Tansy, rolling her eyes, followed.

Gwyneth wandered among the trees, cutting across the even rows as if a piece in a living chess game.

"This one."

The tree before her was tall and slender. She brushed its soft needles, fondling them in her fingers.

Tansy halted behind her. "I like them rounder, so they look more full."

"Yes, but it's going in my house. It'll fit perfectly in the corner by the hearth."

"Your house, your choice, Ma. The Scotch pine it is."

They wrangled the tree off the field. They thanked the men who tied it to the roof of Gwyneth's car, then drove to Gwyneth's house for lunch and tea.

Liam was in his garden when they arrived. He was wearing an

oversized coat, gray corduroys, and Gwyneth's scarf. Gwyneth took a deep breath and watched him for a moment in silence.

"Is he there?" asked Tansy, noticing her mother's attention. She leaned to the side to see him around the bend of the house, then clapped her gloved hands excitedly.

"Let me go say hello," she said, laying her hand on her mother's arm. "Then I'll help you with the tree."

"I don't want to leave the tree on top of the car."

"It'll be fine! You should come say hello, too. Hey, what's up with you guys? You used to be pretty tight, but I haven't seen you talk to him lately."

"Oh," said Gwyneth, looking away. "I've been busy."

"Well, I'll be right back. The tree will be fine for five minutes."

A half hour later, Gwyneth was still watching out the window as Tansy held a basket full of yellow berries—elderward, from what Gwyneth could tell—for Liam as he picked them from the vines. Gwyneth studied Liam for any sign of affection toward her daughter. He certainly didn't seem to be saying much. Tansy appeared to be talking. Every so often Liam would stand there and listen to her, nodding occasionally, sometimes even laughing.

Eventually they brought the basket inside. Tansy waved as she exited the barn, glancing at him over her shoulder and then sauntering off, her sensual figure gliding over the snow.

Gwyneth hurried from the window and sat on the couch, swiping her book off the table, expecting Tansy to emerge at any moment. When a couple of minutes passed, she laid her book on the table and cautiously approached the window again.

She couldn't see anything, but she heard voices coming from the driveway. She peeked out the front door, only to find Tansy and Liam cutting the tree from the roof of her car.

Her heart sank. She considered hiding upstairs until the tree was inside and he was safely gone; instead, she stood to meet them, nervous tingles in her belly, her heart threatening to burst as she heard them bumbling awkwardly up the porch steps.

Taking a breath, she opened the door to allow them inside.

"I would have helped you," said Gwyneth as Tansy, holding the top of the tree, shuffled inside. Liam, with the trunk, followed just behind.

"That's okay," said Tansy, directing Liam to the corner of the room, where Gwyneth had already prepared the tree stand. "Liam's big and strong! He doesn't need any more help."

Occupied with the tree, which he was now placing in the stand and pushing to an upright position, Liam did not respond to this. He cautiously removed his hands from the tied-up tree, then stepped slowly back, making sure it was even.

"Perfect!" said Tansy, clapping.

Liam nodded, exhaling from the exertion.

Gwyneth felt her stomach rise up into her throat. "Thank you for your help," she managed to squeak, the sound of her pulse pounding in her ears.

Liam glanced backward for the briefest of moments. "Oh, sure, sure," he said, nodding again. "It's no problem."

Gwyneth stood frozen for a moment or two, then cleared her throat. "Well, let's cut the ties," she said, attempting carelessness, though her voice shook. She pulled a pair of scissors from an end table drawer. "You do the honors, sugar."

"Hey, Liam," said Tansy, taking the scissors from Gwyneth's outstretched hand. "Check out the tree skirt. Isn't it beautiful?"

"Yes," said Liam. "Did you knit it, Gwyneth?"

He was picking the discarded string from the floor, and hadn't looked at her.

"Yes." Oh, how she hated smalltalk—how pointless, and empty, and false. "I made it many years ago, when Tansy was just a little girl."

"It's lovely."

"Voila!" exclaimed Tansy, standing back as the tree came to life. Its branches now free, it stood lush and proud. Gwyneth smiled despite herself.

"It smells wonderful," she said, relaxing a moment.

"Yes," said Liam. "It certainly does."

Gwyneth regarded him longingly. "You're wearing my scarf."

"Oh. Yes." He glanced down at himself and took the scarf in his hand. "Yes, I am." He looked at it a moment, then smoothed it against his coat. "I like this scarf. It's a very good scarf. You were very kind to give it to me."

He was staring at the tree, his expression blank. He turned to the women, but didn't look at them.

"Well, I'd better be off," he said, tossing the string in a wastepaper basket by the desk. "It was nice to see you both."

"No, Liam!" cried Tansy, her body slumping in an exaggerated fashion. "I thought you'd stay and help us put up the ornaments."

"I can't." Liam pushed up his glasses, still looking at the tree. "I have to get back to the elderward."

"Oh, the elderward will be there in an hour. Please stay."

"I'm sorry, Tansy. I really have to go. But thank you."

"Are you sure?" Gwyneth ventured, surprising herself. "We'd love to have you."

Liam looked at her for a long moment. "I appreciate that, Gwyneth." He smiled then, and Gwyneth's heart was crushed. "I really do. But I have to go."

The women stood there as he waved and walked away, closing the door gently behind him.

"Well, that was nice," said Tansy, leaning over the boxes of ornaments Gwyneth had carried down from the attic. "Too bad he couldn't stay. He's so busy with that silly garden. I asked him a couple of times if he wanted to go out, but he says he's been working every night. Hasn't he made enough *jam* already?" Tansy laughed playfully. "Say, where are the lights?" She looked about for a moment or two. "They must still be in the attic. I'll get them." She rose and walked toward the stairs, deliberately nudging her mother with her elbow as she passed.

Gwyneth wasn't listening: she was stepping toward the

window, where she peered outside, not even caring if she was visible. Liam was back in his garden. The basket was on the ground, and he was kneeling in his elderward, harvesting the star-shaped fruit. As she watched, he pulled the scarf tighter, double wrapping it and pulling through the ends until it covered his chin and mouth. If he saw her standing there, he didn't let on. Gwyneth watched him for a minute, until Tansy called her back. Then she closed the curtain and joined her daughter at the Christmas tree, a new memory coming alive with every ornament they nestled among the garlands.

CHAPTER ELEVEN

*M*ore days passed. Gwyneth felt every minute of them, as if they ran together without distinction or end. They seemed empty without Moriander's garden, without her sense of purpose, without her friend. Gwyneth missed him deeply, her partner in the goddess's harvest. She longed to tell him that for a brief period, she'd felt important, powerful, and free; she wanted him to know she saw his goodness, that he was lovely inside and out. She saw him harvesting, heard him reciting his poetry at midnight. But shame and disappointment had dampened the joy she'd found in these things, and she shunned her window, pulling the curtains tight.

About a week before Christmas, Gwyneth couldn't help but notice activity picking up in the barn. He was receiving packages again, and he was making more trips from the house to the barn, evidently preparing his shop for the grand opening.

"Is he opening the shop on the twenty-fourth?" Gwyneth casually asked Tansy as they cleaned up from dinner one Saturday night. A pang of regret tugged in her gut as she thought about the ceremony she would have performed with him the night before.

"Yes! Isn't it exciting? Maybe now he'll have more time for a personal life."

"He'll probably be even busier, sugar. Running a shop is a very time-consuming job. Besides, you should be excited for him, not yourself."

"Of course I am! I should take him out to dinner to celebrate."

Gwyneth scrubbed the inside of her pot with a little more force than necessary. "It's impressive that you're not giving up on him. Given how busy he is, I mean."

"Actually, you know, Ma, he's really super sweet. I have to admit I'm surprised how much I like him. Anyway, I don't have anything else going on right now, you know? Might as well see where this goes!"

Gwyneth said nothing, letting Tansy ramble on.

Later that evening Tansy disappeared while Gwyneth was switching out her laundry. Suspecting her next door, she didn't go in search of her. She sat on her loveseat by the fire to wait, her knitting in hand.

Tansy's cell phone rang from the table, and Gwyneth ignored it. When it rang a second time a minute later, she rose to look at the screen. Frowning, she put on her coat and boots, took the phone in her hand, and stepped outside with her heart in her throat.

The door to the barn was ajar. Gwyneth knocked warily. Pushing it open, she saw Liam and Tansy lining up jars of jam on the shelves along the walls. They were engaged in light conversation; Tansy was laughing. As Tansy placed the jars beside each other, one by one, Liam discreetly straightened them until they were in a perfect even line.

Gwyneth knocked a little louder. Liam and Tansy turned.

"Oh, hi, Ma," said Tansy cheerfully. "Look how good it all looks!"

"It's beautiful," Gwyneth agreed, indulging in a moment to

take it all in. "It's a real shop." The jam shone in the fairy lights, the colors bright like a rainbow. All around, signs in elegant script labeled each jam and explained its story, quoting stanzas from the poems they'd recited in the garden. Cloth had been draped over tall display tables, softening the room with waves of white.

"Do you want to help us?" asked Tansy.

"Oh." Gwyneth came to attention, recovering from her awe of the room. "Actually, I'm here to tell you that Aunt Molly called you twice." Molly was her late mother's sister. Gwyneth had had a contentious relationship with her mother, and she rarely spoke with her mother's family, but Molly often relied on Tansy for help calling insurance or scheduling appointments. "I didn't know if it was important."

"I was supposed to call her!" Tansy smacked her hand to her forehead. "I'll call her from the car. It's getting late anyway." She placed her hand on Liam's shoulder. Then she stood on tiptoe and kissed his cheek. Liam blushed furiously.

Tansy embraced her mother. "I'll talk to you tomorrow."

"Okay," said Gwyneth as Tansy rushed out.

Gwyneth and Liam stood frozen as Tansy's footsteps pounded up the steps of Gwyneth's front porch, then pounded back down as she ran to her car. A moment later, headlights lit the night, and through the half-open door they heard Tansy peel out of the driveway.

Gwyneth turned to Liam, who turned to Gwyneth.

"Congratulations," she nearly whispered. She swallowed and spoke more loudly. "On the opening. I guess it's happening on schedule."

"Yes." Liam watched her with a sober expression, then smiled and turned back to the shelves. "I'm really happy to be on schedule."

"You must have been working so hard."

"I have. Tansy's been a big help."

Gwyneth's eyebrows rose high. "Really? That's good to hear. I would have thought she'd be more inclined to stand there and talk while you did the bulk of the work."

"She has," Liam confessed sadly, then turned back to her and laughed. "I'm so sorry, Gwyneth. I know she's your daughter. She's really very nice, and I appreciate her trying. But boy, can she talk my ear off."

Gwyneth joined in his laughter. "I was wondering how you were managing. She's a great help with the dishes and such, and her intentions are good. But she isn't generally one for back-breaking work."

"No." Liam's laughter subsided. "How..." he began, and pushed up his glasses. "How have you been?"

"Good." Gwyneth frowned, and her chest suddenly ached. "Actually, not good at all."

His face instantly turned serious. "Why not? Are you okay?"

"I miss you."

He stared at her intently, his eyes wide and alert.

"I..." he began, and stumbled. "I don't understand."

"I just mean...that I miss you." Gwyneth felt tears rising. "I mean that I miss you so much."

He relaxed his stance as he studied her, shoving his hands in his pockets and turning to face her fully.

"I want you to understand," she told him, wiping her eyes on her sleeve, "that I didn't say to you...what I said to you...because I wanted to."

He furrowed his brow. "Then why did you?"

Gwyneth smiled ruefully. "Because Tansy said she was interested in you."

His brow now rose, and he straightened further, appearing taken aback. "Tansy? Interested...in *me*?"

"That's right."

"Wow." He looked downward, appearing to consider this. "I had no idea. Really, we're so wrong for each other."

"I know."

He looked at her then, and his voice gentled. "But why didn't you just tell me? I would have understood." He smiled kindly, melting her. "We could have worked it out together."

"I didn't want to betray her confidence. I've made so many mistakes with Tansy. I just..." Tears threatened to overwhelm her; she paused a moment to collect herself. "I just couldn't deny her anything."

Liam approached and embraced her, pressing her tight into his chest.

"I thought I had done something wrong," he said, and Gwyneth sighed at the comfort of the vibrations in his chest. "I thought maybe you didn't feel the chemistry in the kiss. Or worse, that I'd offended you somehow."

"No, no," she said, wiping her eyes again as he released her. "It was nothing like that."

Liam stood close, facing her; his nearness was reassuring and safe. "Maura always told me I was coming on too strong. Even when we were married. She said I didn't give her enough space." He took a deep breath. "Sometimes I have trouble reading signals, so it didn't seem so hard to believe. I was nervous about making you uncomfortable."

"No." Gwyneth smiled tearfully at him. "You never did, or could."

"The last thing I'd ever want to do is offend you."

"I know that, Liam. I know."

He said nothing for a few moments, watching her as she sniffled. "I'm sorry if I've caused any trouble."

"Oh, Liam. You're no trouble at all. You're the opposite of trouble."

A brief silence passed.

"I missed you, too," he whispered.

She looked up at him, her vision hazy with unshed tears and the halo of fairy lights. They leaned in toward each other, tentatively at first, a hand on an arm here, a rise of the chin there; they moved ever closer, until mere inches separated their hurried breaths. Gwyneth exhaled and closed her eyes. When his lips touched hers, she tilted her head, spurred to take him deeper at the sound of his eager sigh. She wrapped her arms around his neck, her arms grazing the scarf she'd made him, which he'd worn every day since. His fingers in her hair, his breath intertwined with hers, Gwyneth let him consume her, feeling needed, and loved, and alive. They broke abruptly, holding each other and panting, unsaid words hanging heavily in the air. With tender smiles, and a laugh of relief, they locked up the barn and scurried through the cold into the house.

It was dark inside, the only light that which shone weakly from a lamp on the entryway table. They discarded their coats and hung them on the coatrack, then faced each other in the darkness, neither brave enough to meet the other's gaze. Gwyneth was conscious of the strangeness, this nighttime meeting that had happened so many times before, and yet never exactly this way. Her hand lifted momentarily, as if to reach for him, but it lowered almost of its own accord, seemingly frightened of its own exercise of agency. In response, his hand lifted brusquely, as if willing itself not to falter, and landed on her shoulder, his energy evident in the gentle but firm pressure of his fingertips. Gwyneth rewarded his initiative by stepping closer to him, until magically, her hands were on his face and she was kissing him without restraint, spurred by the clutching of his fingers against her skin. In a moment, they were stumbling up the staircase, and into a bedroom bathed in glistening moonlight; though they'd undressed for each other many times in the garden it now felt new, and thrilling, and full of sublime magic. His hands gripped and squeezed her; Gwyneth melted at his sighs. She whispered his name and accepted his kisses, her own hands exploring him as her eyes once did. Beneath his touch, skin glimmering in the moonlight, she was a goddess in worship, beautiful and pristine. Emboldened with power and passion, she deepened her kiss, drawing from his throat a deep, hoarse moan. Then they fell into each other with joy and freedom, the steady starlight seeming to bless them from above.

CHAPTER TWELVE

Gwyneth and Liam woke Sunday morning to find snow drifting by his bedroom window. The world outside was subdued but illuminated, an effect only new snowfall can achieve. Soft light just barely glowed over the windowpane, just as the moon emits the merest hint of a shine.

In this hushed, serene atmosphere, they lay tangled together, limbs indistinguishable beneath a mess of sheets. Shifting subtly together, exchanging kisses, they relished the cozy intimacy, blithely oblivious to the time that passed, warm and vibrant in their snug embrace while the landscape slept in a blanket of white. Gwyneth sighed with contentment. In this room, in this bed, in his arms, was a pure, perfect peace. She closed her eyes to absorb it. Her fingers toyed with his ear, and he smiled, repaying her with a kiss.

He was stroking her face with his fingers, a drowsy smile on his lips and his hair mussed adorably. Gwyneth couldn't stop looking at his eyes, which without his glasses were even more enchanting. With their complex earthy colors and their thoughtful depth, they seemed to offer her a glimpse into the center of the Earth itself.

She grinned as he snuggled in closer, his hands on her back pressing her tight and his lips nuzzling into her neck.

"If it's all right with you," he said, "I'd like to just stay in bed and do this all day."

"It's all right with me."

He leaned over her and took her in a kiss. Gwyneth shifted her leg to accommodate his hip and slinked her arms around his back, eliciting from him a slow, silent sigh.

"It feels like a dream," he breathed.

"The best dream," she whispered, and neither said any more.

Eventually they rose for breakfast and coffee. They sat cozily across the kitchen table from each other and chatted as if they'd been waking up together every morning for years. They were just indulging in a second cup of coffee when a cardinal startled them by pecking at the kitchen window.

Liam turned to her with a smile. "Cardinals are supposed to be a sign or a signal. I've read they're actually loved ones sending messages from the beyond."

"Mmm," murmured Gwyneth. "It must be here for you, then. I don't have anyone who would send me a message from the beyond."

"I wonder if it's Grant giving us his blessing."

Gwyneth froze. "Yes," she said, forcing herself to sip her coffee, hoping he couldn't sense the thumping of her heart. "Yes, Grant would do that. Of course."

Around noon they decided to harvest some berries. Gwyneth returned to her house briefly to fetch her snow things. Then the two of them went into the garden with a basket, which they placed between them as they pulled the fruit from the vines.

It was a quiet, magical time, snowflakes falling all around them, coating the garden in a soft white veil and softening the sounds of their movements. Gwyneth turned to him and smiled. What a kind, earnest man he was. She adored the way his floppy brown hair peeked from under his simple knit hat. His eyes were intent on his work, and his cheek was rosy with cold. On a whim, she leaned over and kissed it. He looked up with a smile and kissed her on the lips.

She turned to him fully and embraced him; he wrapped his arms around her waist. They exchanged happy kisses in the snow, until the sound of a car door jolted them apart.

Gwyneth turned to find Tansy standing between their houses, her arms straight, her mouth agape. As Gwyneth watched her, she turned on her heels and stormed back toward her car.

"Tansy," called Gwyneth, scrambling to her feet. "Tansy, wait!"

"I can't believe you," said Tansy. "I seriously can't believe you did this."

She'd opened the door of her car; Gwyneth held her arm.

"Please, come in the house with me. Come in the house so we can talk."

"Why, so you can justify betraying me? No thanks."

"Tansy." Gwyneth's voice was unusually firm. She stared at her daughter with a frown. "You're coming into the house with me. Now."

Tansy firmed her jaw and slammed the car door shut. She followed Gwyneth up the steps and into the house.

"So you two are thing now?" asked Tansy, pulling off her gloves and coat.

"Yes," said Gwyneth, removing her coat and hanging it on the coatrack. "At least, I think so."

"Did you sleep with him?"

"That's none of your business!"

"I'll take that as a yes."

Tansy shook her head and, hands on her hips, stalked to the other side of the living room.

"Tansy, I'm sorry." Gwyneth approached her, but stopped halfway across the room. She realized, then, that she was afraid of her daughter, that after so many years of worrying about her, she was intimidated by her, too. "I would never deliberately hurt you."

"You slept with him, Ma. Even after I told you I was interested."

"I'm sorry."

"And he's, like, half your age!"

"No, he's not." Gwyneth bristled. "He's only twelve years younger. And besides, you told me I was still young."

"Not *that* young!"

Gwyneth was stung, and her frown deepened. She was beginning to sense this was going to be even worse than she'd feared, that she was about to find herself on the wrong end of her daughter's fiery temper. She watched her, speechless, trying to formulate words.

"I just feel so betrayed. I'd finally found someone *good*. And you inspired my interest! You're the one who's always telling me to find someone nice."

"Come on, Tansy." Gwyneth's heartbeat was increasing steadily. "You never really liked him. He's just not your type. And he never even expressed any interest in you."

"Well, I was working on it! He was always so nice to me, I'm sure he would have come around."

"And what then? Even if it had worked out, how long would you have stayed with him?"

Tansy turned around swiftly. "What's that supposed to mean?"

Gwyneth felt tears rising. "Nothing, Tansy. Nothing."

"No. I want to hear you say what you mean."

Gwyneth saw this taking a downward turn very quickly. She firmed her quivering lips. "I don't want to have this conversation."

"You mean you don't want to say out loud the things you've been thinking for so many years."

Gwyneth closed her eyes and said nothing.

"Well," said Tansy, her voice firm with defiance. "You're going to say them. Because I'm not leaving until you do."

Gwyneth opened her eyes. She knew instinctively this would end in the moment she'd feared for close to thirty years. That it was here, finally, after so much effort to postpone it, was surreal. Gwyneth's relationship with Tansy flew through her mind in an instant, a relationship that was about to shatter into pieces. It was going to happen; she was going to lose her daughter, the most important part of her life. She took a long look at her, knowing she may not have the chance to do so again.

"Tansy," she began. "It's just that...I mean that...I didn't see the point of not...Because you drift from one man to the next. Nothing is ever serious."

"It's not an excuse. And I don't appreciate the subtle criticism. I mean, so what? Maybe I like to be with different men."

"It wouldn't be such a bad thing if you didn't want to settle down. But you do, and that's what bothers me."

"Who the hell cares if it bothers *you*? It's my life. No one asked you for your opinion."

"But you do, all the time. We sit there in the kitchen and you cry over men you've lost."

"You are so judgmental." Tansy shook her head, her face dark. "I've always known it, you know. You don't want to say it, but I hear it in your voice. It's the same tone you use when you're talking about nursing school."

"I don't judge you," said Gwyneth, her voice more strong. "I only want you to be happy."

"You know what it is?" Tansy stood with her weight on one leg, her hand planted on her hip. "I figured it out. You just want to force me into what you yourself couldn't have."

Gwyneth was taken aback. "What...what do you mean?"

"It's so obvious. You missed out on the perfect family. You want to live vicariously through me."

"That's ridiculous."

"I guess I shouldn't even blame you. Daddy was so special, you could never hope to replace him. You must have figured you could never meet that standard."

Gwyneth said nothing. Her heart was pounding so hard she

began to shiver and shake. She desperately wanted to sit down but couldn't make her legs move; she opened her lips to respond but couldn't find her voice.

Tansy seemed to sense her conflict. "Ma?"

Gwyneth hardened herself. "There's something I have to tell you."

Tansy's eyes widened with fear. "About what?"

"About your father."

Tansy stepped backward, frowning. Her eyes grew tearful as if she knew the pain she was about to receive.

Gwyneth took a deep shaky breath and spoke. "Your father," she said, surprised by the evenness of her voice; after all these years of fearing it, telling the truth seemed to free her of a monumental burden. "He wasn't who I told you he was."

Tansy was silent and still. Gwyneth went on.

"You thought your father and I met at the beach." Gwyneth laughed, in release, and also at the absurdity of this lie. "I told you that because I couldn't bring myself to reveal the truth to my sweet little girl."

"And the truth is?"

"That your father was more than twice my age, a filthy rich executive with a wife and four children, who paid my family off to keep his identity a secret."

"Oh, my God." Tansy sank into a nearby chair and leaned forward, holding her head in her hands. "Oh, my God, Ma."

"I didn't intend for it to happen," Gwyneth went on. "I'd only told you he had to go away, that he couldn't be with us. Then one day, I was having a hard time. I was young and lonely and scared, and I'd been thinking of how I'd been used. I was fed up, and I said your father was dead to me." Gwyneth couldn't control her shaking. She took a deep breath to calm herself. "You thought I meant he was dead. You asked how he died, and I told you he drowned in lies." Here she was overcome with tears. "You didn't understand. You asked me how he drowned. I said he was chasing a girl, and you thought he saved a girl at the beach from drowning."

Tansy was running her fingers through her hair, shaking with silent tears.

"I let you believe that," said Gwyneth. "It seemed to make you feel better to think he was a hero. I never corrected you. At the time, there didn't seem a point."

Gwyneth waited for Tansy to say something, but Tansy continued crying in silence.

"I tried to shield you from a father who didn't want you. I thought I was doing the right thing. He saw you once and had no interest at all. You were, and are, much better off without him."

Suddenly, Tansy raised her head and looked at her; panic shone in her eyes. "Ma," she said, with poorly controlled terror. "That picture of him. It's really him, right?"

"No." Gwyneth closed her eyes again, unable to bear the sight of her daughter's anger. "No, it's not."

"Then who is that a picture of?"

"Tansy." Her eyes still closed, she shook her head. "It's a picture of Van Donnelly."

Gwyneth couldn't see Tansy's response, but she heard her angry crying. Continuing to shake with both fear and relief, Gwyneth stood there, waiting for her daughter's rage.

"You bitch," Tansy ground out. Gwyneth opened her eyes to find her face as dark with hatred as she'd expected it to be. "All these years you let me think that was my father. Van fucking Donnelly. You made a total fool out of me. I feel like a joke. How did this even happen? Why Van Donnelly, of all people?"

"I met him once when he was on location in Portland. I kept the framed picture in my bedroom." Every word of this confession pained her; she blushed furiously, feeling humiliated. "One day you asked me who he was, and I said I was in love with him. You assumed he was your father. It went downhill from there."

Tansy laughed darkly and muttered under her breath. She

once again leaned forward, and her hair fell before her, her hands now hiding her face.

"It isn't your fault." Gwyneth's voice was hoarse; lord, could she use a glass of water.

"Damn right it isn't. It's completely your fault. Every last bit of it."

"I'm sorry." Gwyneth began to feel calmer now that the worst of it was out. "I really was trying to protect you."

"Sure, you were. You were protecting yourself. So who was he? Who was my real father?"

"Well," said Gwyneth, her anxiety renewing, and bracing herself for the second blow, "for starters, his name was Jack Ballinger."

"Jack Ballinger." Tansy spit the words out slowly as if they tasted vile on her tongue. She closed her eyes and began crying all over again. "Then why Grant?"

"Grant Jones..." Gwyneth's voice shook; suddenly, it seemed even more absurd than ever. "Grant Jones was the name of Van Donnelly's soap opera character before he was famous."

Tansy threw her hands in the air in exasperation, then shook her head and laughed bitterly.

"You never looked him up?" asked Gwyneth, already regretting the words, but unable to stop herself. "It didn't seem like a coincidence?"

"Of course it did!" Tansy's voice resonated through the room. "Of course it seemed like a coincidence. What do you think, I'm fucking stupid? You told me this lie over more than twenty years. Why would my mother lie to me? Over something as important as this?" Tansy's tears renewed; she wiped them violently away with her sleeve. "You were—you were my hero, Ma. My lifeline." She closed her eyes and sobbed. "I thought you were perfect. I thought you could do no wrong. I still do." She paused a moment as she gasped for breath. "Yes, it was a coincidence. But I had no reason not to believe you."

Gwyneth's tears fell in silence as her heart split open and shattered into pieces.

"Why Grant Jones?" Tansy's voice was cold as ice. "Why?"

Gwyneth had never felt more mortified. She feared she might be sick, but she pressed on. "I had to give him a name. I always had a thing for Van Donnelly, when I was a girl..." Her voice trailed off, and she shrugged meekly. "It seemed as good a name as any."

Tansy laughed bitterly. "That's the dumbest thing I've ever heard."

"It wasn't to me." Gwyneth didn't think she'd ever felt smaller in her life. She sucked in her breath, forcing back her emotion. "I was so young, Tansy. I had a tough time. It was a small relief, to pretend."

"Grant Jones, Ma! Grant fucking Jones! How could you let me believe this?"

Tansy took a few deep breaths, and Gwyneth did the same. Finally Tansy spoke, her voice reflecting her exhaustion.

"Whatever happened to him?" she asked. "To my real father. To Jack Ballinger."

"Sugar," said Gwyneth, softly. "He died."

Tansy began crying again. "When?"

"About fifteen years ago."

Tansy sobbed loudly, and Gwyneth gave her time. She bit her lip as she watched her daughter suffering. That was the most painful part, that her lies had prevented their meeting. It was the part for which she had the most regret, the part of which she was most ashamed.

"You kept him from me." From behind her hair, Tansy's voice raged. "All these years I wanted my father. I could have contacted him. I could have even met him."

"He died of a heart attack without any warning. It was sudden, for what it's worth."

"It's not worth anything. Why does it even matter?"

"If you had been older, I would have told you. You were just a teenager. You weren't ready yet."

Tansy had stopped crying; she looked at Gwyneth with an expression she'd never seen before. She was like a frightened caged animal, with fiery determination in her eyes. "Don't make excuses," she seethed. "You're trying to make yourself feel better."

"I'm not," said Gwyneth. "It's the truth. I always wanted to tell you before it was too late."

"You didn't tell me because you were embarrassed."

"I mean, yes, I was embarrassed." Gwyneth shifted uncomfortably where she stood. "I was very young when I was with Jack. He was a friend of my father's. He seduced me one night at my parents' own house." Gwyneth firmed her heart as the memories of those weeks came flooding back in a rush—memories she'd suppressed and pretended hadn't happened, that had molded her into the woman she was regardless of her determination to deny them. "He sat next to me at their dinner table. He put his hand on my knee. I wasn't a child. But I was young, too young. I knew it was wrong, but part of me was excited. This strong, powerful, handsome, rich man. He wanted me—me! A man who had the world, who had all the money he could dream of. He had a beautiful wife and a huge, expensive house. And yet." Gwyneth was surprised by the force of her anger; she heard it in her voice and felt it in her blood, being unlocked from her heart after all these years. "I was a small, quiet girl from an influential family. I never lived up to my parents' demands. Jack made me feel special, at least at first. And I guess part of me did it to get back at my parents."

"That's pathetic."

Gwyneth raised her eyebrows with surprise. "You think it's pathetic?"

"Totally pathetic. You let him use you. You let him get you pregnant."

"You don't understand." Gwyneth's voice hardened as she

defended herself; she crossed her arms in protest. "It really wasn't my fault. He was rich and powerful, in a position of authority. When I started to pull away, he…he made me feel so low, like there was something wrong with me for resisting him. He gave me expensive presents…He convinced me I was ungrateful. You just aren't in control of these things. You just can't always speak up. Especially at that age, especially three decades ago."

"I don't want to hear your sob story. You're an adult at nineteen. You could have just said no. You were in college then, right? You should have known better."

"No." Tears sprang to her eyes again, this time not in pain, but in anger. "He had too much power, Tansy. He truly did. You're young, maybe you don't yet see it. But men, they teach us we're nothing, that we're there for their pleasure, that—"

"Oh, spare me the feminist bullshit!" Tansy now stood and faced her. "I'm a hundred times more feminist than you! At least I don't take shit from men. At least I can move on. You criticize me for having a lot of relationships, but take a look at yourself. You're claiming complete lack of agency. You've barely dated since. That was almost thirty years ago! At least I leave when I see it isn't working. At least I have some self-respect."

"You don't take shit from men?" Gwyneth's eyes stung with tears; she was brutally hurt by Tansy's accusations, but put them aside, seeking to hurt her in return. "You stayed with Ken when you knew he was married. You were ready to destroy that family. And he kept coming back, and you kept taking him."

"At least I finally left him. I didn't have a child with him, then lie to the child about his existence."

"Tansy, you were so ready to believe it, I couldn't tell you the truth. You wanted so badly to worship that man as a hero. You'll still believe anything men tell you. You still don't see their flaws."

"Don't you dare judge me. Not after all this. You've always looked down on me for having so many relationships. You've never understood that maybe I just like men."

"God, Tansy!" Gwyneth was nearly maniacal, the emotions becoming too much. "How many times have you cried at that table? How many times have I assured you one day, something would work out? Yes, I lied about your father. Yes, I've been a lousy role model. But I've always taken good care of you. For much longer than I should have had to."

Tansy's mouth dropped open; she closed it, her face scrunched with pain. "And that is possibly the most hurtful thing you've said to me. Don't talk to me like I'm a child. You've let me cry at your table. Okay! I've always been there for you, too. Who comes over in the middle of the night for tea, when you're sad and you don't know why? Who comes home every holiday, knowing you have no one? Who's encouraged you for twenty years to get out there and date again, because she can almost taste your loneliness, because she can't stand to see you unhappy?" Tansy stomped toward the door, where she threw on her coat, scarf, and gloves. "I thought we were helping each other; I thought we'd grown to become friends. I didn't realize that you were babying me, that you saw my dependence as weakness."

"Tansy, you can't leave when we're fighting. It's not fair."

"Damn right it's not fair. Goodbye, Ma."

And with that, Tansy left, and it was over.

CHAPTER THIRTEEN

*G*wyneth stood frozen for a very long time, allowing her heartbeat to return to normal speed, giving herself time to absorb what had just happened. For nearly thirty years she had guarded these secrets; she'd always been aware that neither telling the truth nor burying it could guarantee a happy ending. Every day that had passed had found Gwyneth more anxious, for every day she withheld the truth was another day she'd confined Tansy to a false identity. Tansy would never meet her father, because of her. She'd lived a lie every day of her life. It was a decision Gwyneth had made knowingly, willingly, eagerly. And now she would pay the price.

Gwyneth sighed and rubbed her face in her hands. Would Tansy ever forgive her? That, she didn't know. Even if she did, the relationship was wounded. Tansy could never trust her again, or confide in her without fearing Gwyneth's judgment.

Had she been too harsh on Tansy? Had she been judging her all this time? Was her desire for Tansy to find romantic security a reflection of Tansy's desires, or of her own?

Gwyneth found herself questioning not just her relationship with Tansy but also her relationship with herself. She'd been lying to Tansy, yes. But had she been telling herself lies, as well? Was she as judgmental as Tansy had said—as old-fashioned, as conniving—as weak?

Gwyneth didn't know the answers to these questions, but one thing, she knew for sure. With resigned calm, she slipped into her coat, then walked next door to Liam's house before she could talk herself out of it.

He was no longer outside; the basket of berries had been brought into the house. She knocked on the door firmly. Emotion simmered inside her, but she knew what she had to do, and ordered it to remain contained.

He answered the door almost immediately, as if he'd been waiting for her to knock. "Hi, Gwyneth," he said, his face tense with concern. "Are you okay? What happened?"

"Am I okay? Not really. I mean, I guess I am, in some ways. Can I come in?"

"Of course." He swiftly stepped aside and let her through, then closed the door behind them. "Can I make you some tea? I made some with the hollywot berries. It's a lot sweeter than you'd think."

"Oh. No, Liam, I'm sorry." Gwyneth smiled despite her despair. "I can't stay for tea. I just have to tell you..." She swallowed back tears. "I just have to tell you that I just can't see you again. For real this time."

Liam watched her in silence for a moment. "Are you sure?" he asked, with what was clearly contrived calm: though he kept his expression neutral, Gwyneth couldn't miss the dismay in his eyes. He tried to smile. "I was hoping we could talk about how to figure this out."

"No." Gwyneth shook her head. "I can't mess this up; I can't hurt my daughter again. I've already made too many mistakes."

"But," he began, and stopped. His expression turned so imploring, Gwyneth had to look away. "But being together wouldn't be a mistake."

"I know." Her voice was a whisper. "But I can't do it, just the same."

Liam didn't say anything; he seemed to be trying to simultaneously let her take the lead, and convince her to change her mind.

"But, can I ask you," he pressed, ever softly. "What do you think is the point? What I mean is, what would it accomplish, for you to make this decision?"

"Because Tansy feels betrayed. And I've already betrayed her."

"You wouldn't be betraying her." Liam's voice gentled even further. "I wouldn't be with Tansy, even if it wasn't for us. To be perfectly honest, I'm uncomfortable being passed back and forth. Can't you let me make that decision?"

"I can't let her feel betrayed, even if the betrayal is imagined."

"Gwyneth." His voice was beginning to sound desperate. "I can't imagine she's still...*interested* in me. Not after all this."

"It doesn't matter." Gwyneth was beginning to grow exhausted. She inhaled deeply. "This is about Tansy and me."

Liam looked away, and Gwyneth gave him his moment. Oh, how she would miss him, his gentle strength and his honest smile, his eagerness to immerse himself in something beautiful and good.

"I lied to you, Liam," she said suddenly, and he turned to her once more. "Tansy's father—Jack—didn't die a hero. He was a wealthy businessman, a town fixture, an associate of my father's. He was twice my age and married." She rubbed her lips together, holding back tears. "I lied to Tansy all these years. I lied to you, too. I didn't have to, but I did. It was easier for me, at the time."

The warmth in his expression almost undid her. He cocked his head in sympathy and gently stroked her cheek.

"I've lived in this house since Tansy was a baby. Jack set me up here, because it was isolated and out of the way. My parents disowned me after it happened. It was only years later that they let me back into their lives."

"I'm so sorry," Liam said, resting his hand on her shoulder.

Gwyneth took a breath. "Growing up, I learned ballet, and violin, and Latin. I went to charm school and wrote calligraphy. But I never measured up."

"No," he said, his voice heavy and low. "The fault was with them, not you."

Gwyneth smiled mildly, but then sighed again, and frowned. "I have such guilt over that family. Over his wife and his children." Her voice began shaking, and she took a deep breath, steadying herself. "The things his wife said to me when she found out." Gwyneth closed her eyes and shook her head with the memory. "I deserved it," she whispered. "I still do."

"You don't. It wasn't your fault. Please don't talk about yourself this way."

Gwyneth inhaled shakily and exhaled, trying to find her peace. "I'm sorry I lied to you."

"Gwyneth." His eyes were shining and bright; Gwyneth found comfort there, despite her pain. "You don't have to apologize to me. I understand why you did it."

"I wish I hadn't disappointed you, too."

"You didn't. You never could."

Gwyneth ran her fingers through her hair; he rubbed her shoulder in a soothing, even rhythm.

"I want to be with you," she said, her voice shaking. "But Tansy is my daughter, and I love her."

"Yes, of course." The motion of his hand stopped, and his eyes now glistened with tears. "But I love you."

Her own tears clouded her vision of him. "I love you, too," she whispered.

They stood motionless for quite a while, neither wanting to unsettle the other. Finally Gwyneth straightened and sighed.

"I really should go," she said as she reached for the doorknob.

"Gwyneth. Wait." He'd reached out to stop her. Gwyneth could see his mind working as he tried to figure out how to convince her to stay. "Um. The ceremony. The Ceremony of

Twelve. It needs two people. I realized it last night." He attempted a smile, but his eyes were wide and desperate. "Maybe you wouldn't mind helping. With the ceremony. That's all. Just with the ceremony, perhaps?"

But Gwyneth was shaking her head. "I'm sorry, Liam. I just can't. You should do it yourself, though. I know how much it means to you."

"I don't want to do it without you."

"You should do it. Please, please do it." Gwyneth rubbed her face in her hands and looked at him with red, weary eyes. "I wish you all the best with your shop. I'm sorry to have brought you into this."

"I understand." His face was clouded with grief; Gwyneth turned away, unable to bear it. "If you change your mind, please don't hesitate to tell me."

"I won't change my mind, but I appreciate your saying that."

"Gwyneth." His hand on her arm stopped her from leaving; his face was resigned, but grim. "You're a good person. You are. I just think you deserve to be happy."

"I've destroyed my relationship with my daughter. I don't deserve happiness, or love."

She opened the door and went home.

CHAPTER FOURTEEN

*G*wyneth lay awake in bed that night for a long time, her head turned as she stared out the window into the moonlit night. Her head on the pillow, she could see the top of Liam's house, the tall snow-capped turret that contained so many beautiful secrets. In another universe, perhaps, they'd be sitting in the turret at that moment, conspiring together and reading poems no one else would understand. She'd be looking forward to another visit from her daughter, when over tea and cookies they'd chat about topics that had nothing to do with anyone's problems. No one would be lonely, and feelings would be uncomplicated. What made this universe so elusive, anyway? It really didn't seem like all that much to ask.

But in another universe, Gwyneth wouldn't have squandered thirty years. She would have made hard decisions then to avoid hurting everyone around her now. She wouldn't have stolen her daughter's father. She wouldn't have stolen her life. If she hadn't shattered her daughter's trust, she wouldn't have been cut by the shards.

Gwyneth was now truly alone, without family or friends and, most importantly, without her daughter. The loneliness she'd thought she'd felt for decades was nothing compared to this. It was more than loneliness: it was misery, it was emptiness, it was a dark shroud suffocating her soul. Her life no longer held meaning. She brought no joy to anyone, only chaos and pain. She did not deserve the happiness she extinguished in those she loved.

Gwyneth slipped out of bed and shut the curtains, then climbed back into bed and fell into a restless sleep.

AT WORK the next day Gwyneth supervised activities with a sixth-grade class researching Dearham buildings. Each team was tasked with gathering facts about various establishments in town. Gwyneth divided them into groups and designated them to tables, which she'd prepared with laminated copies of historical photographs and documents. One team was researching the post office, another, the ice cream parlor. Other teams were researching the general store, the old primary school, and the Historical Society building itself.

Gwyneth answered questions and made herself put on a smile. Though she usually enjoyed working with children, today her heart wasn't in it. She wandered from table to table mechanically, without seeing, forcing herself to snap to attention when students asked for help. Their shyness and innocence charmed her, and she gradually felt their smiles draw her from her gloom. Soon, engrossed in their eagerness, she was able to forget her worries, and she welcomed the distraction.

The students left, and the rest of the day was quiet. Leona asked her what was wrong and offered to take her out for coffee after work, but Gwyneth politely declined. Five o'clock came, and they locked up the building and left, Leona to have dinner with her husband, son, and grandchildren, Gwyneth to the silence of her cold empty house.

GWYNETH PULLED up her driveway absentmindedly, thinking she'd make the most of her quiet evening by curling up in front of the fire with a good book to help her escape. When she saw the car already parked there, her heart leaped with almost unbearable joy. She halted suddenly and put her hands to her face, releasing a long breath. She inhaled again, as if she'd been without air all day. Her relief overwhelmed her. She was practically shaking as she turned off the car.

As she opened the door, her joy was tinged with fear. She didn't know what Tansy intended to say to her. She didn't think she could handle another confrontation. She stepped out of the car and shut the door, the movement triggering Tansy to do the same. Gwyneth noticed the box of cookies, the string of which was dangling from Tansy's fingers. The two women faced each other in silence for a long, tense moment, until Tansy stepped forward.

"I love you, Ma," she said, frowning. "I don't want to fight with you."

Overcome with tears, Gwyneth went to her, and the two embraced tightly before pulling apart and looking at each other.

"Thank you," Gwyneth gasped, out of breath. She hadn't lost her daughter; it was going to be okay. "Thank you."

"Can we go inside and talk?"

"Yes. Yes, of course. I'm sorry. I'm sorry. Thank you."

She pulled Tansy close again, holding her tight.

"I said some harsh things to you," said Gwyneth. "I'm sorry."

"Whatever, Ma. You were mad. I was too."

Gwyneth exhaled with gratitude. She closed her eyes and rubbed her daughter's back. "I told him I can't see him anymore." A wave of sorrow rushed her, threatening to renew her tears; it tightened her heart, making it difficult to breathe, but she swallowed it back. She looked at her daughter and forced a cheerful smile. "So that problem is solved."

"Yeah, I want talk about that. Inside." Tansy smiled and patted Gwyneth's shoulders. "Come on. These cookies aren't going to eat themselves."

They went into the house, stomping the snow off their boots. In the kitchen, Gwyneth put up the tea kettle, and Tansy pulled the string from the cookie box. Once settled, they sat at the table. Gwyneth fell heavily into her chair, looking at her daughter frankly.

"It was my fault, sugar. I shouldn't have lied. You're right, it was selfish. Well, part of it. Whatever pain I've caused you, I am so, so very sorry."

Tansy was watching her with a sad little smile. "I said some things I shouldn't have, and I'm sorry, too." She sighed. "Anyway, it's okay. I understand why you did it."

"I don't even understand why I did it." Gwyneth closed her eyes and remembered those days, just the two of them, she and her little daughter against the whole entire world. "You deserved the truth, but I was too weak to give it."

"You're human." Tansy fiddled with the handle of her teacup, thinking. "Honestly, in your shoes I might have done the same thing."

Gwyneth's eyes softened. "You really think you would?"

"Sure." She chuckled. "What woman wouldn't prefer to have been with Van Donnelly instead of some rich loser who hung her out to dry?"

Gwyneth ventured a smile. "I guess that's true."

"In all seriousness." Tansy's face turned solemn. "I'm still processing this. It might be a while before I really feel okay. I hope you can understand that."

"I do."

Tansy sat thoughtfully for a moment or two. "You know...I think on some subconscious level I suspected there was more to the story. It hurt to hear it. But somehow it wasn't a total surprise."

"It wasn't?"

Tansy was frowning as she watched her finger absentmindedly trace the edge of her plate. "You and I know each other pretty well. There was sometimes...this look...in your eyes as you talked about him. It wasn't anything I could put my finger on. But just the same." She shrugged. "I let it go because I thought I imagined it. I guess I just wanted to believe it, as you said."

"Putting myself in your shoes, sugar, I understand why you'd want to."

"And putting myself in your shoes...I get how you could have gotten too far into the story to go back."

Gwyneth bit her lip as tears swam in her eyes once more. Tansy handed her a napkin, and she dabbed at them, nodding.

"You know," Gwyneth said, after she'd pulled herself together, "the thing I'm most sorry about is the effect it had on you. I feel like I made you vulnerable. All your searching, your quest for the perfect man." She took a deep breath as she calmed. "You've gone so long thinking he exists."

"Ma, part of it's just my personality. You know that."

Gwyneth smiled tearfully, then frowned. "I've just made so many mistakes. And not just with you. I shouldn't have let him get to me as he did. I knew it was wrong, and I did it anyway. I've felt so much shame for so many years."

"Well, if it wasn't for your so-called mistake, I wouldn't be here, so I'm glad you made it. Aren't you?"

Gwyneth began sobbing. She put her head down to compose herself.

"Yes," she breathed. "Best mistake I ever made."

They sat in silence for some time, their teacups steaming cozily between them. Finally Tansy leaned forward and took her teacup in her hands, staring into it.

"I've been thinking a lot about what you told me," she said.

"About my father—about Jack. I understand that, too." She picked a cookie from the box and nibbled on it, now leaning back in her chair. "You were pretty damn young. What you said about how powerful he was, about how he made you feel when you resisted. That makes a lot of sense."

Gwyneth nodded in silence.

"I've been in situations like that, too. You know, where you feel overpowered." She looked at her mother solemnly. "He took advantage of you."

Gwyneth met her gaze with sad, serious eyes.

"Men in this world," Tansy went on. "Sometimes they feel entitled. And I think we instinctively believe it. You know? Isn't that what we're taught?"

"Yes." Gwyneth's blood sparkled with something special, something wonderful and new—the putting to words of thoughts she'd always had, the female connection to the woman closest to her in the world. "Yes, it is. I'm just sorry I fell for it."

"Hell, Ma, we all do. You fell for the charms of a handsome, powerful man. If that's a sin, I'm a hundred times more guilty than you are."

They laughed a little, and Gwyneth relaxed, now nibbling on a cookie and appreciating its indulgent sweetness.

Tansy continued, "But you know, it's made me stronger. I like men. But I don't need a man. That's why I get rid of the ones who don't work for me."

Gwyneth stopped eating and looked at her. "You're absolutely right," she said. "Thank you for putting it that way."

"There's something else." Tansy looked at her mother frankly. "I told you I don't want to go to nursing school anymore. I need you to be okay with that."

"I am," said Gwyneth, with a somewhat heavy heart. She made herself smile. "I can be."

"You need to understand that it's just not who I am. I know

you wouldn't want me to do something that wouldn't make me happy."

"I wouldn't," said Gwyneth, sincerely. "I definitely wouldn't. It's just..." Gwyneth frowned and sighed, then smiled sadly. "I don't want you to be lost," she said softly, her voice shaking.

"I know that." Tansy placed her hand on her mother's and leaned in intimately. "But chasing a dream that's no longer mine is no way to get found."

Gwyneth sniffled and rubbed her nose with her other hand. Tansy passed her a tissue.

"Tansy," said Gwyneth, once she had calmed. "I don't care if you go to nursing school. I really, truly don't. I only wanted it because I thought you wanted it. I let circumstances dictate my life. I wanted more than that for you."

"I get that." Tansy played with the string of the cookie box. "I'm not opposed to doing something different. The Salty Seashell's fine, but I know I can't do that forever."

"What do you think you want to do?"

"I don't know." Tansy slumped in her chair, thinking. "I mean...I guess what I'd really like to do is home design."

Gwyneth sat up straighter and looked at her daughter wide-eyed. "Oh?" She thought for a moment, the wheels in her mind turning. "I think that's a fabulous idea!"

"You do?"

"Sure. It's something you've always been interested in. I think you'd be great at it."

"Hmm." Tansy held her chin in her hands, staring into her tea. Then she looked at her mother with a look Gwyneth had never seen before: her eyes, round and wide, sparkled with excitement. "I think I'll look into some programs."

"I think that would be wonderful."

They sat for a few moments, thinking.

"Ma," said Tansy.

Gwyneth looked at her. "Yes?"

Tansy's eyes were glassy with tears. "Can you tell me about him? About my father?"

Gwyneth swallowed. "Of course," she whispered.

"He was an asshole," said Tansy. "But I'm still compelled to ask."

"As you should be." Gwyneth took a deep, preparatory breath. "Well," she said, "he really was so handsome."

Tears rolled down Tansy's cheeks, and she wiped them with her hands.

"He didn't really look like Van Donnelly," Gwyneth continued. "Maybe if Van Donnelly were lighter-haired and taller. And if he wore a suit. Jack always wore a suit. Suits aren't really Van Donnelly's style."

"Not bad," said Tansy, nodding with approval. "What else?"

"He was a hedge fund manager from Boston, and he and his family owned a house here in Maine. He and my father were work associates. That's how they knew each other."

Tansy was watching her, taking it all in. "Was he nice, at least on the surface? Did he smile a lot?"

"Yes, and yes. He was friendly with me, and he made me comfortable. He never treated me like I was so much younger. I guess that was part of the problem."

"How old was he?"

Gwyneth hesitated. "He was forty-six at the time."

Tansy's eyes widened, but she didn't respond.

"You might recall my telling you he had children," Gwyneth continued. "That means—"

"—that I have half-siblings." Tansy's eyes had widened further. "That didn't even occur to me."

"If you want, I'll help you find them."

Tansy teared up again. "Really?"

"Of course. But only if you think you can handle it."

"I do. I definitely do. Thank you."

They nibbled their cookies, gathering their thoughts.

Gwyneth relished this familiar, comfortable activity, eating her favorite cookies in the company of her daughter. The normalcy was so welcome, only more so, because no secrets lurked in the corners.

"Ma," said Tansy. "I hope you don't mind my saying. But I think you should get back with Liam."

Gwyneth dropped her cookie and stared at her, blushing. "No, Tansy, no. I don't want to talk about that."

"Well, you're going to." Tansy's eyes had turned sly. "The more I think about it, the more I see how perfect you are for each other."

"It isn't happening. So you might as well stop thinking about it."

"Don't not be with him on my account. You were right, I didn't even really like him. I mean, I like him just fine." Tansy pulled another cookie from the box. "He's super nice. For you. Not for me."

Gwyneth rubbed her lips together, shifting in her seat from the queasiness in her belly. "I just don't think I can do it."

"Why not?"

"Because I'm scared."

She was as equally surprised as Tansy to hear these words come out of her mouth. She said nothing more, contemplating what she'd just said.

"But..." Tansy furrowed her brow. "What are you afraid of? You know Liam's a better man than my father. Than Jack." Tansy frowned. "I don't know what to call him."

"You should call him whatever you want to. It may take time to figure out what that is."

"Mmm." Tansy studied her mother. "So what are you afraid of?"

Gwyneth sighed, absentmindedly running her finger along the rim of her teacup. "When I got pregnant...I felt so powerless. I saw how foolish I'd been, how he'd never really loved me. The excitement seemed so silly. I was so ashamed." Gwyneth paused a moment to go back in time, to remember how she'd fully felt her youth then, how suddenly she realized how manipulative he'd been. "My parents were furious, and they cut me out of their life. Jack discarded me. He acted like nothing had happened between us, like he was the victim. He paid them to keep it a secret. He *paid* them." Gwyneth looked at her daughter, fiery anger in her eyes. "As if I were rented property."

"How awful."

Gwyneth took a sip of tea and went on. "I realized I'd misread him. And I saw how I'd been used. It made me feel...differently... about men." She teared up here, and paused again. She hadn't fully grasped how deeply this had affected her.

Tansy was watching her with compassion. "But Liam's not like that."

"I know he's not." Gwyneth blew her nose, trying to collect herself. "But I feel...I don't know." She leaned back in her chair and looked up toward the ceiling. "Dirty? Undeserving? Weak? Small?"

"You're none of those things. You raised a daughter with no help at all. You made me feel loved, you kept me fed, you made sure I was a good person. All by yourself. You did that, Ma. *You.*"

Gwyneth's lower lip had begun quivering; at Tansy's last words, she sniffled and shook, giving way to the rest of her unshed tears. Tansy held her hand across the table as she did so.

Tansy's voice was low and gentle. "You can't spend your entire life making yourself miserable over one mistake. A mistake you made when you were a teenager. A mistake that gave you your best friend."

Gwyneth lowered her chin and smiled at her daughter. "You think I should forgive myself?"

"I think you should. And I think you should consider that you're allowed to be happy."

"It's very hard to be trusting. I wish I could be as trusting as you."

"And I should probably exercise a little more caution."

"I guess we even each other out."

"I guess so."

They smiled at each other. Gwyneth was rejuvenated. Suddenly, nothing else mattered, nothing but what was happening at that table at that moment.

"Maybe we don't need men at all," she said.

"Well, we don't need them, but they sure are fun." Tansy laughed, and Gwyneth laughed, too. They clinked cookies, smiled, and moved on to lighter topics.

CHAPTER FIFTEEN

*L*ife returned to normal, or at least, to the normal Gwyneth had known before. But nothing seemed familiar anymore; a void seemed to swallow her world, and her old routines were desperately unsatisfying. Nor was she the same person she had been before. She'd danced naked in the moonlight; she'd bidden flowers rise from the snow. She'd unburdened herself of her secrets and rejuvenated her relationship with her daughter, which without the weight of secrecy was strong and steadfast as ever. The illumination she'd gained made the void all that much more painful. And the difference was, whereas before, the void had been nebulous, a feeling of loneliness she'd grown accustomed to and hadn't even known existed, now it had a clear, discernible shape. She sensed its presence constantly, and everything she looked at, she saw through its lens.

It was painful for her to observe his preparations for the shop's upcoming opening, but she couldn't escape them: the twenty-fourth was fast approaching, and visions of him were everywhere. He was outside early in the morning when she left for work, harvesting the garden; in the evenings, he was setting lights up on the outside of the barn, and Gwyneth suffered a tender tugging in her heart as she remembered her first glimpse of the beautiful scene he'd created inside. From her window at night, if she wanted to, she could peek through the curtains and look at them, the delicate fairy lights that now hung in uneven half-moons around the building, inviting guests to enter. They twinkled in the darkness and reflected in the snow, making the winter white landscape seem to glow with intrigue and mystery.

Gwyneth tried to avoid watching, but she couldn't help herself. She wanted to be there, to be a part of it, to be a part of him. She sighed inside at the sight of his familiar movements, his lanky frame, his well-worn clothing, his finger pushing up his glasses. Was it wrong of her to watch him so, in secret? To remember what he felt like wrapped around her, how his fingers felt as they'd gripped her, how his lips had felt beneath her ear? When he was a stranger, she hadn't given her spying a second thought. Now it felt an invasion, as if she'd forfeited the right to this intimacy. Still, she watched him; it provided the only connection she had. She wondered if he saw her everywhere, the way that she saw him. She wondered if he thought of her in random moments of the day. He appeared to be so busy, she doubted he had time.

Several times she considered walking over, to offer to help him, at least. She was sure he could use the help. But she was embarrassed and afraid, and she never did. Instead, she watched from her window as he tended to their garden all by himself. Eventually there came a point when too much time had passed. Even if she'd been able to find the courage to approach him, she'd be too ashamed to do it.

❧

GWYNETH FELT she was a shell of herself—or worse, a new, fuller version of herself, but stuck in her old self's life. It was a cage she'd willingly constructed, and she supposed she deserved the pain it caused her. She consoled herself thinking it was probably for the best. She'd hurt him too badly; she'd rejected him twice. Probably he'd never take her back. And if he did, he'd probably never trust her. If she were in his shoes, she probably wouldn't either: she'd been hurt thirty years ago and hadn't trusted any man since.

Leona noticed her dejection, and let her wallow for a while, and then one day confronted her.

"I know what this is about," she said, scrunching her paper coffee cup in her fist. "Peaches hasn't been around here in ages." She tossed the cup across the room; as always, it missed its mark and lay on the floor beside the trash can. Mr. Harlowe, seated at the table in the corner, followed the cup with his eyes. When it fell to the floor, he looked up at Leona and gave her a thumb's up.

"Good try, Leona! You almost made it that time."

Leona muttered under her breath.

Gwyneth smiled and turned to the old man in the corner. "How's your work going, Mr. Harlowe?"

"Very well! I'm almost done!"

Leona snorted. "You've been almost done for twenty years."

"But this time, I mean it!" exclaimed Mr. Harlowe. Leona mouthed the words along with him.

"Mr. Harlowe," said Gwyneth, "I admire your fortitude. This is something you've done for yourself, because you enjoy it. And you haven't let anyone or anything stop you from doing it."

"Why, thank you, Miss O'Shaughnessy." Mr. Harlowe cast her a glowing smile. "Anything worth doing is done with passion!"

"I know someone else who feels similarly," said Leona. "Don't you, Gwyneth?"

"Yes." Gwyneth disregarded this comment and turned the page of the little packet on her desk. The sixth graders she'd tended to the other day had handwritten her thank you notes. Some had drawn pictures of the town, of the historical building, or of her. She couldn't help but smile as her eyes took in their handwriting. They were not quite children, but not yet adults. They were shy, innocent, and adorably deferential. Gwyneth enjoyed when classes visited the Historical Society; the students always seemed to brighten a place submerged in oldness, in the past. She liked how their eyes looked when they perused pictures of their town long ago. She hoped another class would visit soon.

"Miss O'Shaughnessy," said Mr. Harlowe, sifting though the papers on the table, "do you remember that book I was looking at the last time I was here? I seem to have misplaced the title."

"It was Matthew Lamkin's book," said Gwyneth, rising to fetch it from a bookshelf against the wall. "The Depression-era mayor."

"That's right!" Mr. Harlowe beamed at her as she glided toward his table and laid the book before him. "My dear, I don't know what I would have done all these years without you."

"It's all right," said Gwyneth, smiling and patting his shoulder. "That's what I'm here for."

"Well, your kindness toward a silly old man is appreciated."

"You're not silly," Gwyneth protested. "You're hard-working and sweet."

"Ah, stop it! You're making me blush."

Gwyneth chuckled and returned to her seat.

"What are you doing for Christmas, Mr. Harlowe?" asked Leona, pouring herself a cup of water from the cooler in the corner.

"Not sure, yet," said Mr. Harlowe as he perused the book Gwyneth had brought him, his eyes squinting behind his glasses.

"Your daughter isn't coming to see you?" asked Gwyneth. She put down the papers she was holding and frowned. "You can't spend Christmas all alone."

"Rose is due to have her baby any day now." Mr. Harlowe now raised his eyes and looked at her, his face suddenly glowing. "She doesn't want to travel in her condition. And I can't drive all that way by myself anymore."

"Mr. Harlowe, I'll be home on Christmas, with my daughter Tansy. If you're all alone, I'd like you to call me. You can spend your Christmas with us."

"That's sweet of you, dear. Thank you. I will."

"Gwyneth," said Leona, waving her hand for Gwyneth to join her. "I'd like to talk to you for a minute."

Gwyneth turned to her, surprised. "Okay," she said, standing. She followed Leona into the back room.

Leona closed the door behind them.

"Was that unprofessional?" Gwyneth asked. "Maybe I wasn't thinking. But, really, Leona, we're all neighbors here, and I—"

"No, no, I don't care about that." Leona waved her hand again, this time to brush off Gwyneth's comment. "I want to talk to you about Peaches."

Gwyneth blanched. "What? Why?"

Leona stared at her, her face stern. Then she relaxed, sighing and shifting her weight, and the mood grew more intimate. "Honey...I want to say something to you. Not as a boss. As a...well, as a friend."

Gwyneth firmed her face lest she allow in the emotion and totally fall apart.

Leona looked at her frankly. "I see things, you know. I'm not stupid. It was pretty damn obvious you were in love with each other."

Gwyneth bit her lip; the corners of her eyes crinkled despite her best effort to keep her face neutral.

"I'm right, aren't I."

Gwyneth inhaled and nodded.

Leona crossed her arms and leaned against the table. "Mmm hmm. I thought so." She watched her for a second, thinking. "Now, I don't know what happened between you two. There's a reason you aren't together. But what I want to know is..." She hesitated, seeming to change her tack. "Look, we've worked together for over twenty years. I don't think I've seen you happy in all this time."

Gwyneth fidgeted nervously. Was she really so transparent?

"I'm sorry," she managed to utter, her voice nearly a whisper. "I...I didn't mean to be so negative. I'm sorry if I've been a pain."

"What?" Leona seemed taken aback, and her brow creased dramatically. "No, that's not what I mean."

But it was too late. All the pain of the last few days—of the last few decades—was released as Gwyneth saw herself through other people's eyes, a sad, aging spinster with nothing to live for, nothing to give, no real role in life and no achievement of consequence of which to be proud. Gwyneth turned from Leona toward the window, where she could let her tears fall unseen.

Leona rested her hand on her shoulder.

"What's the matter, honey?"

Gwyneth was too moved by Leona's uncharacteristic tenderness to speak, and the two were silent while she composed herself.

"You must've got it bad," said Leona.

Gwyneth took a deep, calming breath and dried her eyes. "It's not just that."

Leona watched her in sympathetic silence, rubbing her back.

"It's just that...well..."

"Spit it out. We don't beat around the bush here."

Gwyneth sighed. "I've just been thinking a lot about...well, about my lack of place in this world."

"What the hell are you talking about?"

The return of Leona's brusqueness felt more comfortable, and Gwyneth calmed somewhat. "I'm stagnant, Leona. I'm forty-seven years old. I'm not going anywhere, I'm not doing anything. I don't do anything at all. When I leave this Earth, it won't be any different for my having been here."

Leona withdrew her hand from Gwyneth's shoulder and stood

with her hands on her hips. "Now, if that's not the biggest load of crap I've ever heard in my life."

"It's true!" Gwyneth faced her. "What have I done, anyway? Who even needs me?"

"Your daughter Tansy, for one."

"Sometimes I think I hold Tansy back."

"Why?"

"Because she still lives here when she could be anywhere she wants to be."

"Tansy's here because she loves you," said Leona. "Because you're her mom."

"Exactly. Maybe she'd have made different choices if it hadn't been for me. Maybe she'd have left this town."

"What's wrong with this town?"

"Well, nothing."

"I rest my case."

Leona was silent. Gwyneth stared out into the snowy landscape to the mountains beyond the forest.

"I still don't see what this has to do with Peaches," she said finally.

"It's just that...I've made some mistakes, Leona."

"Who hasn't?"

Gwyneth rubbed her face in her hands. "I just don't know that I'm ready."

"Look at me."

Gwyneth lowered her hands and reluctantly looked at her boss.

Leona was watching her, her face firm but warm. "You think you don't do anything? You think you don't help anyone? What about those students, the ones who wrote you those cards? What about Mr. Harlowe? What about me?"

Gwyneth stared at her. "Oh, that doesn't count."

"You saying my happiness doesn't count?"

Gwyneth blinked. "Your happiness?"

"Of course. You don't think I've kept you around all these years because you're miserable, do you?"

Gwyneth smiled in spite of herself. "I guess you wouldn't."

"You're important here, Gwyneth. You're important to me. You love this town. You do a good job." She punched her gently in the shoulder. "And you happen to be a good friend."

Gwyneth smiled. "Do you really think of me as a friend?"

"Why, sure."

They stood in silence for a moment or two. Gwyneth stood still, thinking.

Leona leaned back against the table again, studying her. "In all this time, I'd never seen how much you hate yourself. It appears you think you're undeserving, or something. I don't know what happened to you that made you feel that way, but that's some bullshit."

"I don't hate myself." Gwyneth sniffled and pulled herself together; hearing it out loud from someone else's lips was jarring. "I hate that I've hurt people. And I suppose I hate that I've been so weak."

"You aren't weak. You're human."

They stood side-by-side in silence. Finally, Leona nudged her with her elbow.

"Whatever it is, I'm sure he'll be willing to put it behind him."

Gwyneth shifted uncomfortably—she knew that this was true. What she didn't know was whether things could ever be the same, whether she was brave enough to face him now that he'd seen her at her darkest.

"I suppose that's something," she said, "when someone can look past your flaws."

"When you love someone," said Leona, "you don't even see them as flaws."

GWYNETH LEFT work that day feeling marginally better. But she also felt marginally worse, because now, hope of reconciliation with Liam had been renewed. Before, she had resigned herself to unhappiness; she was paying for her mistake, and her time with Liam was simply over. Now that she was considering that her life wasn't as irredeemable as she'd thought, she couldn't escape recognizing the possibility that it was meant to be after all. It wasn't that she didn't want to be with him—quite the contrary. It was that reconciliation would require her to extend her hand, to present herself to him in all her mess and confusion, to make herself vulnerable not only to him, but to herself.

She couldn't bring herself to do it, at least, not that first day. Instead, she sat in the chair by the window, where the light outside the barn illuminated the pages of her book as it rested in her lap. Occasionally, she heard the barn door open and close; her heart would jump, and she'd peek outside, every cell in her body alert and pulsing as she watched him stride between the barn and the house, retrieving this item or that before disappearing once again. Gradually, the pull grew greater than the fear. At some point in the night, in the darkest recesses of her mind, she began wondering if next time would be the time she'd gather the strength to join him.

He emerged again, and Gwyneth sat up straighter in her chair. When she saw him withdraw his key and lock up the barn, she was engulfed by a profound sense of loss. She'd waited too long; she'd missed her chance. Tomorrow, the enchantment of the night would be over.

He climbed the steps of his house and disappeared behind the door. Gwyneth sighed, stood, stretched, and headed upstairs for bed.

The next day was December twenty-third, the day before the opening. At work, Gwyneth couldn't sit still. She was constantly shifting and sighing, and she couldn't concentrate on what she was doing.

Halfway through the day Leona sent her out for coffee.

"Take a couple of laps around the building while you're at it," she told her. "You're as skittish and jumpy as a frightened kitten."

Finally the end of the day arrived. Gwyneth raced home, driving much faster than usual, and pulled into her driveway only to find that in her absence, a sign and been delivered and installed in front of his house.

She couldn't read it because it was covered with a tarp; she guessed he'd reveal it only on opening day. She waited in her car a moment, but he was nowhere to be found. *Just as well*, she told herself, though in her heart, she was disappointed. *If I'm this nervous, I'm probably not ready. I may never be ready. This probably isn't a good idea.*

But all evening long, she thought of him. She knew how excited he'd be, and she yearned to see that excitement light his face. She wanted desperately to be part of it, to know she'd helped him reach his dream. She knew how much more special it would be for him if he had someone to share it with. She knew it because she knew him, and because she knew loneliness herself.

She took a bath to calm herself, with the curtains open to the night. The night was dark; it was a new moon. The stars offered the only light, though they themselves appeared brighter in the blackness.

But she was restless, and she couldn't relax. Her mind refused to be calmed, and her gut was twisting in anticipation. She rose from the water and stood there, dripping onto the floor. The clock in the corner read 11:53. If she wanted to, she still had time.

Naked and trembling, she was overcome with worry. *What if*...but what? He said he wasn't going to do it—what if he wasn't there?...Well, then there was nothing lost, now, was there. But what if he rejected her? What if he couldn't forgive her?...Deep down, she knew these were empty fears; she knew they were excuses. Then what was she afraid of? Was it simply taking the first step? But hadn't she done it before—and hadn't it brought her what she wanted? Gwyneth's body was tingling; she felt power pulsing through her veins. It was several tense moments before she realized that what scared her wasn't worry, but possibility.

Screw that, she thought, rushing to her room. *I'm over standing in my own damn way.*

She blew out her wet hair and dressed hastily, then hurried downstairs toward the front door.

She opened the door slowly and took a deep breath. She stepped onto the porch and into the cold.

A weighty stillness was in the air, like the tense excitement before snowfall. Snow already blanketed the ground in choppy clumps, having been turned up by creatures' footsteps; Gwyneth knew by tomorrow, a new, pristine layer would sparkle in the sun. The snow crunched beneath her boots as she made her way to the garden. Blood racing, she turned the corner around the house, bracing her heart for the sight of him.

He wasn't there. The garden sat empty, and the blossoms stretching from their snow beds were silhouettes in the moonless night. Gwyneth walked halfway across the perimeter, then turned toward the center, toward Aedrian's Star. As she stood there by herself, no poem to recite and no blessing to receive, the garden looked sleepy and unremarkable, like the dormant reeds they were.

She looked about, the sorrow in her heart reflected on her face. She listened intently for the sound of the door, of footsteps marching briskly from the house. Minutes passed. Gwyneth's face and fingers grew cold, and a vast emptiness unraveled inside her, swallowing her heart and leaving her barren. Tears pricked at her eyes, but she did not shed them. She'd been living this life too long; she'd never really expected anything to change. Though she'd lost so much, she'd lost nothing. It was just as well, anyway. She would return to her familiar life, nothing more and nothing less.

Gwyneth looked about at the garden she'd grown to love.

Though simple, it had held magic, had made beautiful things she'd treasured. She sighed aloud, then bit her lip, preparing herself to say goodbye.

Motion in the corner of her eye made her lift her head and start. There he was, his tall frame bundled in his coat and hat, around his neck, the scarf she'd given him. In his typical long strides he silently approached the garden; on seeing her, he halted, standing straight and firm with wide eyes and straight lips.

She exhaled and smiled, relief washing over her as if giving her life.

"You're here," she whispered, her breath rising into the night.

He blinked a few times, then stepped slowly toward her. "You're here," he repeated, his face beginning to soften.

She met him halfway across the garden, by the wonderlore blooms that grew berries as yellow as the sun.

"I..." she began. "I hope you don't mind that I'm here."

"Mind?" he repeated again, brow furrowed. "No." He laughed. "No, no. No, I don't mind."

"I wasn't sure if you'd be here."

"I wasn't sure if I'd be here, myself. I wasn't going to do it. But something made me say, Hey, what the hell." He watched her a moment, his eyes intent on hers. "I'm glad I did."

"Me too." Gwyneth's smile widened; she pursed her lips to control herself. "Um," she said, turning toward the garden, made suddenly nervous by the silence. "Should we...should we perform the ceremony?"

"The ceremony?" Liam stared at her. "The ceremony." Abruptly, as if remembering, he raised his hand up: Llewellyn's book was grasped firmly between his fingers. "Yes, the ceremony. Of course, of course." He cleared his throat and pushed up his glasses. "Let's perform the ceremony."

They shuffled along through the snow back toward Aedrian's Star. The space between them was charged with an electrifying current. She registered every movement he made, every footstep he left with his clunky old-fashioned shoes. She looked about at the garden. Had she noticed, before, how tall the plants were standing, how the shifting shadows of the night seemed to make them come alive? Surrounded by the expectant blooms, she began to feel the magic: it was in the twinkling of the stars, the stillness of the air, the contrast of the white snow against the pitch blackness of the night.

They reached Aedrian's Star and stood together in silence as Liam opened his book to a previously bookmarked page. His hands cradling the book, his head bent, he began to read.

> *The twelfth month, in twice twelve days,*
> *Blooms' roots take hold of Aedrian's stays.*
>
> *At midnight hour, with thine own voice,*
> *In thine harvest thou shalt rejoice.*
>
> *Thou give unto the sacred land;*
> *Thou bestow life with thine own hand—*
>
> *As lovers grow with life anew*
> *And bloom as one, as lovers do,*
>
> *Joined together, not to part,*
> *Joined in root, and joined in heart.*

He closed the book and shoved it into his pocket, then stood utterly still, watching Aedrian's Star in silence. Gwyneth repeated the poem's words to herself, daring to wonder if they held some truth.

She felt it incumbent on herself to speak first. She pushed past the fear and turned to face him.

"I'm sorry," she said, the words seemingly propelled from her chest by her rapidly beating heart. "For everything."

"For what?" He looked at her with his round, kind eyes, and in a moment, Gwyneth saw how needless had been her worries. "You only did what you thought was right."

"But it couldn't have been more wrong." Gwyneth prepared herself to lay down her heart; around her, the flowers seemed to bend their heads to listen. "I've just made so many bad decisions."

"But it's all been to protect your daughter."

"Sometimes it's hard for me to trust my own judgment."

They both looked up: a light snowfall had begun drifting from the heavens. Already it was sticking to their hats and coats. Gwyneth stared for a moment into the sky. It always amazed her how far snowflakes had to fall before they reached the ground.

"But your judgment," he said, so quietly she almost didn't hear him, "brought you here."

She lowered her face to look at him, and a smile touched her lips. "Yes, it did."

A light wind blew, guiding the snowflakes gently sideways so they swirled around the center of the garden.

"You know, Gwyneth," he said then, his face thoughtful and serious, "far be it from me to say anything. But I think...I think you've been doing better than you give yourself credit for."

"I think so, too."

It was so serene out here, so quiet. Gwyneth barely noticed the cold at all. Slowly, she felt the uncertainty seep from her body, unfurling like her breath into the waiting darkness.

"I think I've realized something," she told him, looking at her house thoughtfully. "I've watched people being happy from afar. I...I think I deserve happiness, too."

He seemed to exhale; Gwyneth observed the slow swelling and deflating of his chest. He pushed up his glasses. "To be clear," he began, shifting a little where he stood, "are you saying that you want that happiness, with me?"

"Yes." She smiled fondly at him, her eyes sparkling. "Because, you see," she said, and relented to the tears, "I love you."

He exhaled sharply and smiled. "That's good," he said. "Because I love you, too."

They met in a tight embrace and stood there among the blossoms, which were soft with a dusting of snow. Gwyneth sighed deeply, letting the peace consume her. She herself was late to blossom—but the truth was, she'd given up on blossoming long ago. She closed her eyes and smiled. With the peace came possibility, and with the possibility came excitement. Gwyneth could hardly wait to see where her midnight harvest would lead her.

Her head on his chest, she opened her eyes: his hands had lowered and were rubbing her hips. She lifted her chin, and his lips promptly met hers; a sigh escaped him, and his fingers now gripped her tight. Gwyneth brought her own hands to his shoulders and up his neck, letting her fingertips sneak under his cap and into his hair. He deepened the kiss, and she pressed herself close, then went breathlessly with him into the house, leaving the snow-dusted blossoms to work their magic.

CHAPTER SIXTEEN

EPILOGUE

"Rootberry. Roseberry. Throt. Hollywot. They sound like the names of gnomes or elves."

"Or fairies. Look at this beautiful elderward jam. Isn't it the prettiest pink color? Like a fairy's touch."

Gwyneth handed the jar to a customer, who took it warily in her hands and studied it.

"It is a pretty color," the customer allowed. "But what does it taste like?"

"See for yourself."

Gwyneth reached for a sample jar of jam, then spread some elderward onto a cracker and passed the cracker to the customer.

The customer put the cracker in her mouth. Instantly, her skeptical face brightened with delight.

"That's unbelievably delicious!"

"Isn't it?"

"Where on Earth does this come from? And how much for the jar?"

While Gwyneth answered questions for a cluster of interested customers, Liam entertained a group of Dearham administrators and officials who had come out to take a look at Goddess in the

Garden, the town's newest landmark. A reporter with the local paper also was there. She gazed about her with wonder, her mouth agape at the sight of the fairy lights. She snapped pictures seemingly in a daze, pausing frequently to read the label on this jam or that.

In the corner was a small display with candy made from the herbs and berries from Liam's garden. A group of children eagerly examined it. The candy had been Tansy's idea. It had been the one way she had truly helped him: she'd thought it would excite customers with families, and she had been right.

Tansy was currently on register. She was tending to Mr. Harlowe, who'd hitched a ride with Leona.

"What a pretty collection of jams you've chosen!" Tansy bubbled with amiability as she wrapped up Mr. Harlowe's order. "Are these all for you?"

"No, they're for my daughter. When the baby is born, she'll need some special treats."

"What a sweet, thoughtful father you are." Tansy smiled and reached under the register. She emerged holding a small jar of throt. "Here's a special gift for you, on the house. I know the proprietor. He won't mind."

Liam approached and rested his hand on Gwyneth's lower back.

"Excuse me, Gwyneth," he said, with the lush lilt he always had when he spoke her name. "If you have a moment, there are a couple of people I'd like you to meet."

Gwyneth excused herself and followed Liam toward a couple standing by a display of Gwyneth's scarves and hats. Beside it, shelves of thrown pottery displayed the work of local artisans. The woman was fingering one of Gwyneth's scarves. The man, Gwyneth recognized instantly.

"Hello, Nick," she said, holding out her hand. "It's good to see you again."

"It's good to see you, too. I guess you're getting along with your new neighbor."

"Yes, my neighbor and I are getting along just fine."

The woman turned to them, her face glowing with a wide smile. "I can't believe how gorgeous your shop is. These lights! I'm just beside myself. And what a great idea, to showcase local artists."

"This is my wife Meredith," said Nick. "Meredith, this is Gwyneth and Liam."

They greeted each other and smiled all around.

"Gwyneth knitted everything here," said Liam, rubbing Gwyneth's back and regarding her fondly. "She knitted my scarf, too."

"Your work is so beautiful, Gwyneth. I've always wanted to knit. I think maybe you've inspired me to learn."

"I'd be happy to teach you, if you wanted."

"I would love that."

"Gwyneth," said Liam, "you'll never believe it. Nick and Meredith are thinking of starting a chapter of Building for Hope."

"Oh," said Gwyneth, her brow rising with interest. "Isn't that the organization that builds homes for families in need?"

"That's right. And they're looking for volunteers."

"How wonderful." Gwyneth smiled up at him, her eyes sparkling. "You said you wanted to get involved with a local charity."

"It's the perfect opportunity, isn't it?"

At the end of the evening, they closed the books and straightened up the shop. Tansy kissed them goodnight and went home—she was working in the shop the next morning, and probably would help out most weekends in the future. Gwyneth held her extra tight before sending her off. Tansy squeezed her and whispered in her ear.

"I'm glad you're happy, Ma. Don't do anything I wouldn't do."

Gwyneth blushed and playfully slapped her arm, then watched her pull out of the driveway and off down the street.

Liam met her outside. He locked the door and took her hand, and they walked together toward the garden for a blessed moment of peace and quiet before bed.

"I think the grand opening went really well, don't you?" she asked.

"It went better than I ever could have expected."

They walked the perimeter of the garden, then cut through the center to Aedrian's Star.

"She really does look so beautiful at night," said Gwyneth.

"She does," said Liam. "And Aedrian's Star does, too."

Gwyneth blushed again and wrapped her arms around his waist. He held her close, resting his cheek on the top of her head.

"Thank you for your help," he told her.

"Thank you for yours."

They stood there for some time, holding each other in silence. Gwyneth sighed in sweet contentment. Already this felt right and normal. She was pleasantly surprised by how used to it she'd become.

"So tomorrow is Christmas," she said, pulling back and meeting his gaze. His face was handsome and kind, his eyes wide and bright as the stars. "What do you want to do all day?"

"Why, worship the goddess, of course."

He leaned in and kissed her, blocking out the moon, the stars, and the cold. Gwyneth surrendered, utterly at peace, brought to life in a winter harvest.

THE END

THE MEREDITH SERIES

She's created the perfect life. But when it doesn't turn out as planned, can she take what she's learned and find her way in the darkness?

Meredith Beck had it all: the love of her life, a thriving career, and an apartment in the excitement of New York City. Then tragedy strikes, leaving her adrift in a world that's suddenly lost its luster. Optimistic by nature, she desperately attempts to rebuild. But no matter how hard she tries, she just can't muster her former strength.

Then a light appears in the darkness: Nick Kelly, a quiet painter from a small town in Maine. Thoughtful and kind, and utterly without pretension, Nick is unlike anyone Meredith has ever known. She is drawn to his love of nature and is comforted by his purity of heart. Through his eyes, the world seems to hold limitless possibility, and as their romance blossoms, she's delighted to find herself on the road toward a simpler life, with a partner who reminds her of the beauty in every moment.

But it isn't as simple as it seems. As Nick's own demons surface, the life they're building threatens to unravel. Human fallibilities once again complicate best-laid plans. And it becomes clear that before they can embrace the future, they must confront the lingering ghosts of their pasts.

A story of love, loss, and the power of second chances, *Meredith Out of the Darkness* is first in a slow-burn series of cliffhangers ending with a warm and satisfying happily-ever-after.

ALSO BY AMANDA GALE

ACKNOWLEDGMENTS

A heartfelt thank you to Gina, Jessica, Jocelyn, Sarah, Terri, Dez, Erica, Tamara, Sandy, Melissa, and Katharine for invaluable support, encouragement, and advice.